ANDY McNAB

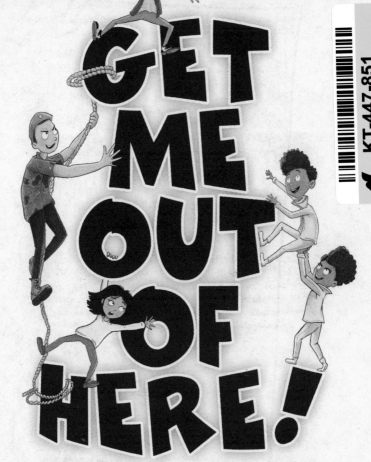

GET ME OUT OF HERE!

PHIL EARLE

ILLUSTRATED BY ROBIN BOYDEN

SCHOLASTIC

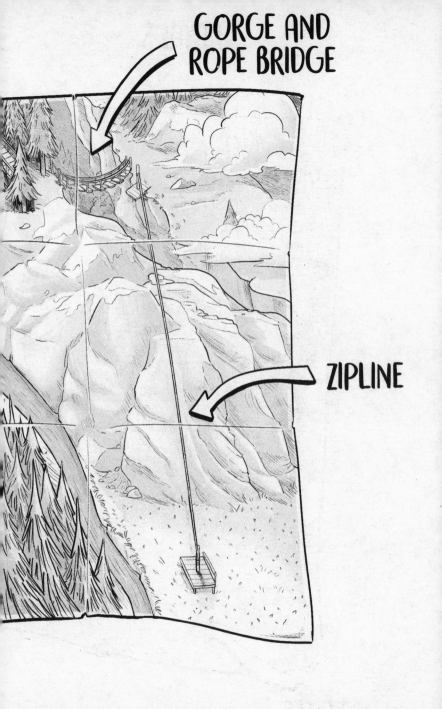

GORGE AND
ROPE BRIDGE

ZIPLINE

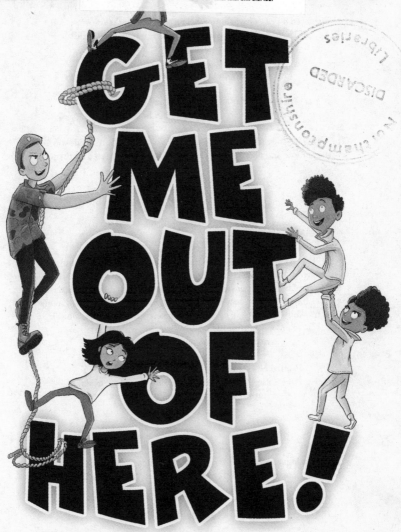

ANDY McNAB

GET
ME
OUT
OF
HERE!

PHIL EARLE

Scholastic Children's Books
An imprint of Scholastic Ltd
Euston House, 24 Eversholt Street, London, NW1 1DB, UK
Registered office: Westfield Road, Southam, Warwickshire, CV47 0RA
SCHOLASTIC and associated logos are trademarks and/
or registered trademarks of Scholastic Inc.

First published in the UK by Scholastic Ltd, 2019

ISBN 978 1407 19568 1

A CIP catalogue record for this book
is available from the British Library.

Printed by CPI Group (UK) Ltd, Croydon, CR0 4YY
Papers used by Scholastic Children's Books are made
from wood grown in sustainable forests.

1 3 5 7 9 10 8 6 4 2

www.scholastic.co.uk

To the team at the Reading Agency who do such brilliant work.

A.M.

To Thomas "Giraffles" Jefferson, Beth Goodyear and all my friends at SBT.

P.E.

"Easy," I tell myself. "Simple. Piece of cake."

Then … I don't move.

Minutes pass. So many that I start to feel sick from nerves.

"Don't be a plank," I say out loud. "You've seen plenty of others do it."

I have as well, kids older and younger, plus I've jumped waaay further myself. Only thing is, those jumps were at ground level, and this isn't.

All right, I'm stood on a brick wall that's only three times my height, but right now it feels like

I'm wobbling on the top of an electricity pylon that someone's plonked at the highest bit of Everest.

So here I am, heart sweating, forehead pounding: it might be the other way around, but I don't know any more. All I know is these two things:

A. I'm not getting down until I jump the gap to the wall opposite.

And…

B. I no longer WANT to jump the gap to the wall opposite.

I should've brought a hat, coat, sleeping bag and pillow up here with me, because by the time I finally do jump it's going to be dark … and cold.

I look down at my trainers, high-tops with built-in swoooosh, made to be springy. The sort of trainers you slam-dunk in.

The only trouble is, my feet aren't the first ones to wear them. At least one other pair lived in them before Mum found them in the charity shop, and now they feel more like concrete wellies than Nike Airs.

The glue holding the soles to the leather probably weighs a few kilos alone, and as much as I love them (second-hand or not) I reckon it'll be these trainers that will see me fall to my death (or at least graze my knee), not the fact that I'm a clumsily short-legged chicken.

My brain does this for ages, whirring and clunking until I'm pulled back to reality by a gentle tap on the shoulder that nearly shocks me off the wall and into the void.

"You jumping or not?" a voice asks.

A voice that belongs to a boy two years below me at school. "Cos if you want, we could go first." He points to another four lads behind him, one of them even younger than he is.

I feel my cheeks flush, like I've been blowing up balloons non-stop since the day I was born. I want to ask them why they aren't in bed yet, or in front of the telly in their 'jamas. I don't say anything, though. Just wave them through, like I'm doing them a favour by letting them get their jump in before their mums call them in.

One by one they jump. All of them make it. One even does it with a spin and I instantly hate him, but also want to be him. Even though he's only eight.

And I have to do it now, don't I? Especially as they're all stood there watching, with big beaming grins on their faces.

I close my eyes and breathe in, then feel a bit dizzy.

Come on, Danny, I tell myself. Then the boys tell me the same.

I open my eyes – it'd be daft to jump with them closed – then count to three in my head, launching off my right foot before I change my mind.

Air rushes past me, and I'm skyward for what seems like ages. I'm going to smash it – probably fly right over the boys themselves. I even get ready to salute as I pass them.

But then something weird happens.

The air turns to treacle and my legs turn to lead. I start falling instead of soaring, and I grapple with the air as if I'm trying to find an invisible ladder that quite clearly isn't there.

The wall's close, but not close enough and, most importantly, my feet are miles from it. No way are they going to land on top. My fingertips do though, biting into the bricks, giving me just enough of a grip to hang on. The rest of me slams into the wall, but I don't feel it. There's not enough room in my brain to know whether I've hurt myself or not.

I can't let go – I'd look like the biggest loser ever. One of the kids even tells me so. Another one offers me a hand but I ignore it, pulling myself up with every bit of strength I have.

It feels like it takes me ages. Like someone could build a wall quicker than I could climb this one, but, eventually, with a grunt so loud it belongs in a zoo, I pull myself on to the top, every bit of me sweating.

It's then that I feel my left leg stinging, then the other one, then my left elbow, then the other one – well, you get the message. Within seconds, my entire body feels like a gigantic graze, but its nothing compared to my wounded pride. Feels like I'd need a million stitches to fix that, especially because the boys are standing over me, pointing and grinning. I notice that most of them have lost their front teeth, which is lucky for them, because I'd happily punch them all out otherwise. Well, maybe if my hands weren't stinging so much.

"Want me to call your mum for you?" one of them asks. I can't tell if he's taking the mick or not.

"No thanks," I say, my voice a lot higher than it was two minutes ago, and I pull myself to my feet.

"Where you going now?"

I didn't even know until he asked me, but now I do know – instantly.

"Back there," I say, pointing at the other wall.

7

"I'm not going in till I land on my feet." And with a hobble and limp, I make my way back.

The boys don't laugh or giggle or point, but they don't stay to watch either. They just shuffle off, one of them saying, "Fair play to him," as he goes, which makes me smile and feel a little bit bigger and in less pain than I am.

I *will* make the jump. Even if it takes all day. Just you watch me.

The day starts like all the others, just as I like it.

I don't need an alarm because the sun wakes me up, belting through the space where the curtains should be hanging, but instead they're lying on the floor, curtain pole still attached. It's like they only fell down yesterday, when actually it was weeks ago.

I tried to put them back up loads of times, honest, but my bedroom wall has got more holes in it than the surface of the moon and in the end I gave up.

Anyway, it means I can suck up the view 24/7. Living on the seventeenth floor is brilliant. The skyline's epic and I can pretty much see everything that's going on out there without anyone being able to see me, which makes me feel like James Bond on surveillance … except I haven't quite got his gadgets, just a penknife with a missing toothpick and blunt scissors. Still, I like it up here.

Breakfast goes the same way as always too, which means trying to duck underneath Dylan as he does chin-ups in the kitchen doorway.

"Fifty-seven … fifty eight," he grunts, though I know there's no way he's done that many. To be honest, I am sort of impressed. I had no idea he could count that high.

"You totting up your brain cells again?" I ask, but regret it immediately as he wraps his legs round my neck and squeezes like a famished python.

"Don't mess with the best," he hisses, "cos the best don't mess."

It's a line I've heard pretty much every day of my

life, and I'm not concerned when the blood pumping in my ears blocks most of it out. I think he heard it in some army movie years ago so rolls it out whenever he can. He even went through a phase of scrawling it on his arm like a fake tattoo, but didn't like it when I volunteered to scrawl it on his forehead instead for maximum effect. I got an extra-tight squeeze that morning, I can tell you.

As per usual, there's only one person who can release me from D's death grip, and that's Mum.

"Dylan, put your little brother down, please," she sighs, without looking up from her phone. She must be able to hear me choking from the other side of the room. Ears like a bat, she has. She doesn't look up when I sit next to her either, gasping and rubbing at my poor strangulated neck. I don't get cross that she's distracted, though. It's not like she's on Facebook or anything; she's looking at the same thing she's always looking at, her banking app, frowning as she does it.

She works like a Trojan, my mum. More jobs

than Dylan can count up to, that's for sure. Most mornings I don't get to see her before school as she's long gone, cleaning first down the hospital before trooping across town to the big offices, where she scrubs up after even more people. She must be amazing at hoovering, the amount of it she does. I just wish she could vacuum up a few of the red numbers that are flashing on her screen. It might make her look a bit less stressed.

"All right, Mum?" I ask.

"Living the dream, love," she replies, though from the bags under her eyes, it looks like the dream is full of rats, vampires and blocked toilets, instead of unicorns, rainbows and five-star living.

"Nice one," I say, before asking for lunch money, which she plucks, coin by coin by coin, from her purse. By the time she's finished my pockets are going to weigh a ton and I make a note not to walk by the canal. If I fall in, that'll be it: death by small change.

"Right, I'm off," she says, kissing my forehead

but not even thinking about doing the same to Dylan, who's doing the most elaborate floor exercises ever witnessed outside a breakdance class. "No joining the SAS before I get home Dyl, you hear?"

"I wish," he grunts, with a far-off look in his eye. "Anything to get away from this loser."

"Play nicely with your brother…"

"Or else?"

"You'll have me to deal with." She smiles. "And remember, don't mess with the best…"

I stifle a snort, loving the fact that maybe it's not just me – maybe she knows just how big a loser he is too. But before I can ask her, she tucks her mop under her arm like it's a rifle and marches out the door, leaving me to follow behind.

I don't want to hang around, the last thing I need is to be used as Dylan's punch bag, so I decide to leave with my nose intact.

8.23 a.m.

Time for school.

And Giraffles will be waiting for me
downstairs.

3

That wasn't a spelling mistake by the way. I know you think it should say "giraffe", like the animal, but don't be getting your red pen out, because Giraffles is actually spot on.

Thomas Jefferson Raffles to give him his full, posh name, though no one calls him that, not even his parents or teachers. Because, by some brilliant coincidence, Tommy was born with a proper, PROPER long neck, leaving him with only one possible nickname: GIRAFFLES.

Don't bother to try and make up any other

gags about him either, because they've already been made:

YES, he always beats the lunch queue by craning his neck to the front of the line.

NO, he never loses in a race because he always wins by a neck.

YES, he can cheat in any test. It's easier to cheat when you can see everyone's answers.

But the best thing about Giraffles is that he's my best mate, and he'll always stick his neck out for me if I need him (in both ways).

I find him in the usual place, waiting by the lift on the ground floor of my block, gazing dreamily into the distance.

"All right, G?" I say. "What you looking at? Juicy leaves at the top of that tree?"

"Yes, mate. Though I wish it was a slice of toast. Woody ate all the breakfast before I even got up."

I nod, feeling his pain. Big brothers are cretins, no matter whose roof they live under.

"You limping?" he asks.

I hadn't noticed before, but my knee is sore, and not just because the lift has broken down again.

"Little bit," I say.

"War wound from dissing Dylan?"

"Nah, bashed my knee up on the wall over there."

"You're not still dreaming of being a free runner, are you?"

"Well, there's nothing else to do round here is there? I haven't got near the Xbox in months, since Dyl saved up for the new Call of Duty, and I'm not much cop at footie am I?"

"But ... *free running*? You have to be mental to do that. Call me boring but I can't see the fun in backflipping off the top of a garage. And anyway, aren't you a bit small for it? Them lads who are good at it are all built like spaghetti and you're more of a baked bean. No offence."

He had a point, but I wasn't going to let him get away with it.

"Maybe you should climb the wall with me.

Then I can use your neck as a bridge."

"Hilarious," he said, though his face said otherwise. He's heard every insult before, after all.

We rest the banter for a while and settle on a bit of moaning instead: teachers, brothers, homework; there's nothing we can't grumble about if we put our minds to it, though to be honest I haven't got much to complain about, other than being too young to do the lottery. A new pair of high-tops with built-in bounce won't buy themselves...

It's not long before the school crowd builds up around us. Marcus and Maureen tag along as always, finishing each other's sentences and reading each other's minds as only twins can.

"Are you limping?" Marcus asks me.

"'Course he is," Maureen answers for me.

"Dylan dead-leg you again?" he asks.

"Not this time," Maureen says, making me wonder if she can read my mind too. Though I bloomin' well hope not, as she's doing my head in right now.

"He's been falling off walls again, haven't you, Danny?"

I nod. No point lying about it, especially if she really is inside my brain.

Does make me laugh though, their names: MandM, you know, like the sweets. And what makes it worse is that their mum and dad are called Mike and Molly. You couldn't make it up, could you? They must've had the rubbishest baby name book going.

Anyway, I try to shut them up about my limp by running at every wall I can see, to show them I have got skills, but to be honest they don't look very interested.

Giraffles' head is in the clouds, almost literally, while MandM are talking in some sort of twin code that could be either highly sophisticated or complete gobbledygook.

Either way, it leaves me to focus on the dream of being the best free runner on the estate, and by the time we reach the school gates, I'm smashing it left, right and centre, front-flipping off postboxes and swallow diving off walls, leaving the lanky spaghetti lads trailing in my dust.

Too bad then that the bell has to go and ring, right at my most triumphant moment. I sigh heavily and file into class. Reality sometimes really does suck.

4

School isn't a dirty word.

Puddle *kind of* is.

Mud *definitely* is.

But school?

Not so much.

Others disagree, they moan about it non-stop, and that's all right, I don't have to listen or anything. I don't have to agree either.

OK, there are bits of it that suck. Whoever invented fractions was a bit weird, and don't get me started on the idiot that came up with conjunctive adverbs (I mean, what even are they anyway?), but there's loads of stuff about school that's all right really.

PE for starters, and history, and that magic twenty minutes every day when we drop everything and get read to. Who doesn't like sticking their head on their desk while someone tells them a story? Weirdos, that's who.

Anyway, school's all right with me. And it's particularly all right this year because we lucked out and got Miss D as our teacher. The teacher every class wanted and only we got. Cue much flossing to celebrate.

Miss D is cracking, in every way.

It's like being taught by someone who is one part mum, one part cool auntie, one part mate and one part encyclopaedia.

She isn't tall. She's real short, which is maybe a big part of why I like her, but she's not a pushover. No way. She's strict when she wants to be, a proper pocket rocket, but she just makes

everything … fun. Well, almost everything. She
makes conjunctive adverbs bearable, which is a
feat in itself.

"All right, Danny, manage to avoid
your Dylan this
morning?" She
smiles as we file in,
finding something
different to say to
every one of us,
whether it's about
new trainers or
what we watched on the
telly box last night.

It makes me grin and feel
good as I take my seat next
to Lucky. Lucky Success.

Never has a
name suited anyone
more. Honestly, it's like he has the Midas touch.
Everything he touches doesn't just turn to gold,

it's like the gold is encrusted with jewels too. And I mean, *everything*.

I swear that boy sneezes diamonds and farts unicorns.

He's the most skilful footballer in school, the best at maths, and has a lighthouse smile that my mum says could charm the birds from the trees.

Lucky lives in the biggest house, with his own room and Xbox, plus his sister's dead lush (tell anyone I said that and I'll put you in one of Dyl's chokeholds), but he's also a good'un, is Lucky. He doesn't milk being ace at so many things, or lord it over you. If he's got a bag of sweets he'll share 'em with you; if he's got a new game on his new phone he's well happy to let you have a go. And that makes him all right by me.

Plus he's smart and he never covers up his answers in a test, which makes him doubly OK. He's a bit too perfect to ever replace old Giraffles, but as a desk buddy I could do a lot worse.

"You get the new battle passes for Fortnite?"

he asks as I sit down.

"Oh yeah..." I reply, though I had no idea there were any. I gave up online gaming months ago. Broadband doesn't exist in our flats. Somewhere in the basement there's probably a hamster in a wheel with a real sweat on, but no matter how hard he spins he's never going to make our internet fast enough.

"We should play online together," he grins.

"Too much free running to do,"

"Yeah, I could see you were still doing that from your limp on the way in."

I feel my cheeks flush as my brain searches for a speedy comeback, but fortunately Miss D interrupts with the register before breaking into what she calls An Exciting Opportunity.

"As you know, end of term is fast approaching..."

Cue cheers from the back row.

"...I know, I know, we're all excited about the Easter holidays. But before we have a well-earned

27

rest from adjectives and long division, something a bit special has come up."

"Have we all won the lottery?" shout MandM at exactly the same time, sending a shiver of freakiness up my spine.

"I don't think any of us would still be sat here if that was the case," beams Miss D.

"Oh no, we're not being visited by the prime minister are we?" asks Giraffles, a question so random it makes me wonder if his long neck has somehow starved his brain of oxygen.

"Hardly, Thomas. I certainly wouldn't be smiling if we were. No, we've been invited on a very special trip…"

Cue groans from the back.

"Please, Miss, tell me we don't have to go to the water treatment plant again?"

"Or to the ruins. Piles of old bricks are well boring…"

I've got to be honest, I wasn't exactly jumping on my seat myself. I think it's some sort of ancient law that school trips have to be:

A. Properly rubbish
B. Properly boring
C. Properly PROPERLY predictable

I knew where we were going: Tickledown Farm. Year six goes there *every year*. Dyl went before he left for senior school. The head makes the oldest kids go with the youngest ones, to "build empathy". But Dyl reckons it was just so the teachers could put their feet up and drink tea all day.

I wasn't so sure. Couldn't imagine Miss D would be up for that either. She looked just as disturbed as us by the smell at the sewer plant.

"I can see you're all incredibly excited by the news. So instead of letting me bore you with the details … why don't you just watch this?"

With a flick of her wrist and a tap on the whiteboard, a film begins. And the second it starts, I feel my pulse race and my palms sweat.

I feel like I'm stood on the biggest bloomin' wall in the world, because on the screen are six beautiful, exciting, eye-popping words:

Are You Ready…

TO GO WILD?

5

"IMAGINE A PLACE..." the voice-over purrs, **"WHERE YOU CAN LIVE OUT YOUR WILDEST DREAMS..."**

I'm already in. I've signed on the dotted line, I've packed my bag and kissed Mum goodbye. What comes next only makes me even more excited.

"Where you can climb the steepest mountains, before jumping from the top..."

I wipe away a bit of spit that's escaped from the corner of my gaping mouth. I can't believe what I'm seeing. The biggest rock face I've ever laid eyes on, so high the top of it disappears into the sky, which is so blue I swear it's been airbrushed by a smurf.

And there, stuck to the side of the rock, is a kid just like me, except with a helmet and ropes coming out of him, and he's smiling like a loon, just like I am now. And though it looks like hard work, it also looks like the best work ever. And there isn't a conjunctive wotsit anywhere to be seen.

The film goes on. And it just gets better, because there's kayaks and rapids, and zip wires and treetop houses, and all the time there's this voice, like the one you hear in a Star Wars trailer, telling me, **"BREATHE DEEP, FASTEN YOUR SAFETY BELT, AND PREPARE TO GO WILD AT WILD OUT!"**

The trailer ends with the sight of a kid zooming down a zip wire at a hundred miles an hour, and as it ends, there's a huge cheer from the classroom, and applause and whooping.

And then I realize that all of that noise is coming from me. And that everyone is looking at me, and laughing and pointing, but I don't care because I've just seen the greatest thing in the world ever, that's better than jumping off any wall, better than a hundred walls that are taller than the Empire State Building. And even though I don't know when we're going to Wild Out, I'm already chalking off the days in my head till we get on the coach.

"You fancy that then, Danny?" asks Miss D, with a smile almost as big as mine. In my head I'm going

to reply with a shrug and a nod and a yeah it looks OK ... but what actually happens is that I throw both hands in the air and shout, as loud as voiceover man himself, **"MISS. I AM ALL OVER IT!"**

Cue more laughter and pointing.

Trips to the water-treatment plant are a thing of the past – this is the future, and the future is so flipping bright I'm looking for the sunglasses just so I don't get an excitement headache.

"I'm pleased you're so pleased," Miss continues. "It really is a wonderful opportunity for us. To visit a place where the landscape is so different to everything we're used to. Make no mistake, it will be challenging, like nothing any of us have ever experienced..."

"Come off it, Miss," laughs Lucky beside me. "We've grown up in the city. It's a jungle *here*. There's nothing in the countryside that's going to scare us. We're hardly going to get mugged by a sheep, are we?"

Others agree. Marcus and Maureen shout, "Too right!" at exactly the same time, while Giraffles looks proper excited as well. Probably because he's thinking about all of the leaves at the top of them tall, tall trees.

"Well, we'll see, won't we," adds Miss D, though her face suggests she knows something that none of us do. "All you have to do, to secure a spot on the trip, is return this letter by a week today, signed by your parents or guardians."

And she hands round the note. I try to read it, but fail. All I can see are the words WILD OUT, which makes me so unbelievably excited that I fear I might actually combust. The rest of the words are swimming in a million different directions, and, anyway, the details aren't important.

All that matters is that I'm going to be on that coach. I'm going to climb everything they put in front of me. I am literally going to be the WILDEST kid they have ever met.

And then I read the sentence that brings me

crashing back down to earth.

"Woah. A hundred and fifty quid?"

Oh.

'Course.

We have to *pay* to go.

My eyes scour the letter, and suddenly the words WILD OUT seem like the smallest ones on the page. The only words I can see, and I can still see them even when I close my eyes in fear and disappointment, are:

Dear Parent or Guardian,

The cost of this once-in-a-lifetime opportunity is one hundred and fifty pounds. Whilst we appreciate it is a considerable sum of money, we are confident it is a trip that none of our students will forget.

Sincerely

I open my eyes, but the words are still there and I can't erase them, not with a rubber, not with a flipping nuclear bomb.

I look around me. Lucky doesn't look worried, but then his dad works in one of them huge offices in the city, doesn't he?

Giraffles isn't sweating either, and neither are MandM, though they are blowing their noses at the same time and making exactly the same noise.

The only person who looks even vaguely disturbed by this gargantuan bombshell is me.

One hundred and fifty quid.

I headbutt the desk in despair.

Going wild?

I won't be going anywhere.

"You wouldn't last two minutes in the wild anyway," laughs Dyl, above the whirring of his hair clippers.

It's one of his most annoying habits (one of many many, many), shaving his own head in the kitchen. I wouldn't mind if he did it over a sheet of newspaper, but he never bloomin' does. Today he's simply leaning over the table, showering the fruit bowl with his greasy stubble. I swear he only scalps his head like this because he's too lazy to wash it.

I cringe, forcing the image of eating a hairy apple clean out of my mind.

Fortunately for Dylan, Mum's paying him no attention: she's still poring over the letter from school, with a huge frown on her face. Normally, she saves that look for when she's reading my idiot brother's report, but today I know it's me causing her grief.

I did think about not showing her it. I could have screwed it in a ball and chucked it in a bin on the way home. At least that way I couldn't keep torturing myself by reading and rereading about a trip I'll never get to go on.

But for some reason, I didn't; I just handed it over sheepishly, with a "Sorry, Mum."

She hasn't said anything since; she just sighs repeatedly and alternates between reading the letter, sighing some more and peering at the banking app on her phone, presumably in the hope that she can magic a hundred and fifty quid from thin air.

In the end, she finally says what I already know.

"I'm really sorry, Dan, but I just can't afford it. Dylan's got cadet camp coming up, plus he's grown about a foot in the last six weeks so he's needed a whole uniform on top." Dyl kisses his bicep and gazes at it adoringly like its Ariana Grande or something.

"I'll pay you back, Mum…" I say, feeling guilty as I say it.

"It's not about that, love. I don't doubt that for even a minute. I just haven't got it to lend you."

"What if I sold some stuff to pay for it? Old clothes, maybe."

There's a snigger behind me. "NO ONE wants to buy your skiddy old kegs."

"I'd sell you if I thought anyone would give me a fiver, but I'd probably have to pay *them* to take you away."

I feel Dyl's response before I hear it: a fist to the back, which really bloomin' hurts, though I refuse to even flinch. His ego doesn't need any inflating, it's already the size of a hot-air balloon.

"Do you think school would let me pay them back then? You know, before the end of term?"

"I doubt it. They're always begging us for donations, so the chances of them stumping up are as small as—"

"Danny's six pack?" adds Dyl, unhelpfully.

What he doesn't realize though, is that every time he opens his mouth, I become more determined. I want to show him I'm every bit as outdoorsy and up for it as he is. That he's not the only one who can climb a rope or save a hostage from behind enemy lines.

It's like Mum is reading my mind too, because from nowhere she pipes up with a lifeline. A twenty-four-carat-gold lifeline.

"Fifty quid," she says.

"What is?" I reply.

"That's what I can give you. For now. Fifty quid. If you can raise the rest, then you can go, Dan. I'd love to stump it all up for you, you know

I would, but unless we give up eating for the next four weeks, that's the best I can do."

I do the maths – a hundred quid.

That's what I have to raise.

In a week.

"Hundred quid," I say out loud, which provokes another scoff from behind me.

"No chance," laughs Dyl. "You couldn't raise a hundred pence." I glare at him while he goes back to shaving his oversized head.

And it's at that exact moment that I know, surer than ever, that I'm going to raise that money. And that my idiot brother, without even realizing, or lifting a finger, is going to help me.

7

"Are you sure about this, D?" asks Giraffles, squirming on the stool.

"'Course I am, mate," I reply. "If Dylan can cut his own hair with these, then I'm sure I can cut someone else's with them."

"Maybe you should start with your own mop, though? Looks like it could do with a trim."

I ignore the insult and focus on where to start. The most difficult bit is making the lead stretch to the top of Giraffles' telescopic neck. I momentarily consider an extension lead, or two even, joined together.

"What style are you after then, sir?" I ask, practising my best customer service.

"None. I'm growing it out." Giraffles makes to stand up and leave, but I push him down with my firm grip.

"You know what'd suit you? A proper David Beckham cut. All shaved and sharp edges."

"Mmmmm..." He doesn't sound convinced, but he doesn't say no either, so I take that as my cue to start, the clippers already vibrating in my slightly shaking hands.

And do you know what? It goes all right. I manage to not chop off his head, and I don't think he even notices when I catch the top of his ear and make it bleed a tiny bit.

The curls fall to the ground, and with every strand I feel my confidence grow. I even start making chit-chat, asking my customer if he's got plans for the weekend or if he's been on holiday lately. I get nothing back though, and I can see

Giraffles knuckles turning white as he grips the leg of the stool.

After only twelve brisk minutes I'm done, and after whipping off the tea towel like a matador's cape, I confidently hand Giraffles a mirror.

He says nothing, though his face does change colour. A lot. First it's green, then it goes deathly grey, and as his eyes burn into the mirror a lot of red starts to appear.

"What have you done?" he yells. "David Beckham does NOT have his hair cut like this!"

"He would if he came here," I reply defensively. "It's the only style I can do. Besides, now you're bald I've just saved you ten minutes in the morning, PLUS you won't have to buy any gel for a good two months."

"I hate it."

"It'll grow back, mate."

"Yeah, maybe, but what about the top of me ear? Maybe we can find that on the floor and glue it back on."

Giraffles sulks, with his arms crossed and everything, for a good fourteen-and-a-half minutes before I shove the biscuit tin in front of him and allow him to graze calmly.

"You're not really going to charge people for this torture, are you?" he says eventually.

"'Course I am. Buzz cuts are proper in at the moment, and most kids pay the best part of a tenner down the barbers."

"But how will people know to come here to get it done? You live nearer the moon than you do the ground."

"Aha, well these little beauties are rechargeable, aren't they, so I'm going to set up my own pop-up shop round the corner from Jack's Barbers. Battery life is two hours and it'll take me fifteen minutes per hair cut, so that's enough for eight customers before I have to recharge. If people pay me four quid a haircut that's thirty-two quid before I even plug back in. I'll have the cash in no time!"

Giraffles doesn't look so sure, and asks to

borrow the wooliest hat I own despite it being the middle of April.

But, a mere thirty minutes later, we're all set up with a kitchen stool, a tea towel, a mirror and a tub of Dylan's gel (so at least it *looks* like I can do more than one style).

I've even painted a sign on an old box, saying

"Spelling error," barks Giraffles.

"It's *urban*," I reply.

"You're an idiot. I give you one haircut and fifteen minutes till you're using that towel to stop your own nose from bleeding..."

But I haven't got time for worrying. This is going to work. It's got to.

And at first, it does! Cos I work out who to target. Kids younger and smaller than me, that's the key. Kids who can't physically hurt me when I scalp them; kids who have a tenner in their pocket from their mum for a trim, and are delighted when I tell them they can keep some of it to spend on sweets.

One by one they perch on the stool, and they don't so much as flinch as I shear them, not even when I get a bit careless with the clippers. Some of them are even happy with what I've done. One kid, who to be fair to him did wear the thickest glasses known to man, even gave me a tip.

After no time at all I have twenty-nine quid nestling in my pocket. If I'd known it was going to be this easy, I'd have set up my business months ago.

But then, there's a glitch. Well, I say a glitch, it's more a gut-emptying horror show of a catastrophe, for as my back is turned, to professionally and expertly blow the stray hairs off my clippers, I get a new, unexpected customer, who is neither younger or smaller than me. In fact, he's bigger than most adults. He's so big, he makes Giraffles look like Thumbelina.

Tubs Wilkinson has taken up residence on the stool, and he's already tied the towel around his tree-trunk neck.

Tubs isn't tubby. At all. *He's ripped.* All over. He's the only teenager on the planet that has a six-pack … on his forehead.

He's not a *complete* thug. Not quite. Though lifting weights twenty-three hours a day does seem to have done something to the way his brain works … and he is known for random acts of extreme violence. Though, happily, never at me … until now.

"Take it all off," he grunts by way of a welcome.

"R-r-really?" I stammer. "But you've been growing your hair for ages."

He has as well. It reaches his shoulders and there's loads of it, proper thick. In fact, his hair looks just like the rest of him: muscular. You could probably knit a rope bridge out of his super-strength locks, I think as I stare at it.

"All of it. And do it quick. I'm due down the gym in twenty minutes. Do NOT make me late."

I have no idea what to do next.

Do I do it, stuff it up and potentially live the rest of my life as a human bruise?

Or do I suddenly develop a chronic wrist injury that ends my promising career as barber to the stars...

"Come on, I'm waiting," he grunts.

So I start up the clippers, step forward, and gulp, even though the tennis ball in my throat refuses to budge...

I am exactly three seconds into the haircut when I realize I am serious trouble.

Tubs' hair is way too long and lustrous for the clippers to make even the smallest of dents in.

In fact, it's worse than that as the hair simply gets locked in the machine's teeth, which grinds and howls before yanking his head back like I've pulled it.

"Nooooooooooooo," I howl under my breath, but fortunately Tubs' neck muscles are so full-on that it feels like nothing more than a playful tug and

53

he keeps his eyes front and centre.

"Quick," I whisper to Giraffles, who's stood wide-eyed beside me, "Hold these. Just for a minute."

He shakes his head so viciously it looks in danger of rolling off his shoulders, and steps back a dozen paces. "I warned you. This was never going to end well."

But it has to. I can't mess this up without my face ending up just as mangled as Tubs' hair, if not more. So I flick the clippers off and leave them clinging to his locks, while I dive into Dylan's toilet bag, which I nicked from the bathroom cupboard.

"Come on…" I mouth, "there has to be some in there, has to be…"

I pull out plasters, unused and otherwise, empty bottles of shower gel and a deodorant that smells worse than any armpit ever did, until, with my heart screaming in panic, I find them: Dyl's nail scissors. They're small and blunt, and appear to still have one of his toenails attached to them, but they are my (and my face's) lifeline.

I return to the dangling clippers, and begin to hack around Tubs' twisted locks.

"Oh yes," I coo, like I know what I'm flippin' doing, "this is really starting to take shape…" And although it isn't, it *is* kind of working, as the clippers fall free into my hand and I continue to cut as much hair as I can from Tubs' head.

I work with speed, purely out of fear, and as the minutes go on, the hair starts to build up on top of my feet. In fact, I'm starting to look more like a Hobbit than an eleven-year-old barber.

Within minutes I've cut the entire left hand side of his head. It's patchy, to say the least, but it's kind of all the same length.

But then, as I snip at the last strand, disaster strikes again.

The scissors – exhausted by a workout that would leave an Olympic sprinter wheezing – fall into two pieces. And no matter how hard I try, I cannot entice them back together.

In my head, I'm wailing and screaming and panicking. Out loud I'm still cooing and bragging about how I'm creating some kind of masterpiece. Anything to not give the game away. But with every passing second I feel more and more out of control, until a little miracle pipes up in my ear.

"Buy yourself some time and get the clippers on the short bit. I'll run and grab some more scissors from home. Mum's got a sharp pair in the kitchen."

In that moment, I could kiss old Giraffles. Well, I say that but his neck's too long to get anywhere near his face, so I settle for a whispered thank you, and turn the clippers back on.

The next three minutes are perfection. The clippers are working, the short hair is coming off easily and I manage not to chop off any part of Tubs' face. It's win, win, win and I smile as I turn my attention to the last bit of unclipped hair. Once that's done, half of the head will be complete. And I know that if I can do one side, then I can definitely do the other.

The clippers slide under the hair at the nape of his neck, but then, nothing happens. Well actually that's a lie. There's a beep, then another beep, then a third beep and then nothing. Because the clippers stop working altogether.

"Is there an issue?" asks Tubs.

"No, 'course not," I lie.

But there is. There really, really is. The clippers are out of battery. And with a sinking feeling I remember that the charger is in the flat, halfway up to the chuffing moon!

I look behind me, desperate for sight of Giraffles sprinting while simultaneously carrying a pair of super-sharp scissors.

At least if I have them I can start cutting the other half. Maybe he'd even sprint up to the flat and charge the clippers while I work.

That would work. Or at least it would if he was anywhere to be seen.

"Come on," says Tubs, pouring yet more panic on top of me. "I haven't got all day."

I try to say something, but all that comes out is a jumble of terrified sounds that are barely words, never mind a sentence that makes any kind of sense.

A muscly arm shoots up in the air. "Mirror," Tubs demands.

"But ... er ... I'm not done yet. Only h-h-halfway through..."

"MIRROR." The voice is louder and full of menace and threat.

"An artist never reveals all until the

masterpiece is complete!"

But Tubs is done with waiting and instead he pulls out his phone and flicks it into selfie mode, and that's it. That's all he needs to see. Suddenly, he's on his feet and towering over me, one half of his head as smooth as a baby's bottom, while the other looks more like he's had an electric shock.

"What's this?" he yells, pointing at his head.

"It's not finished…" I reply, taking a step back.

"Too right it's not. You trying to make me look daft?"

"Course not. It's just my scissors. They…"

"They what?"

"They. Well, they…" I hold them up.

"You've cut my hair with *them*?"

"Er, yeah?"

"They're all rusty … and they're nail scissors!"

"Well, they *were*. I don't know *what* they are now, except junk maybe."

I mean it to be light-hearted. To kind of show how well I've done with rubbish equipment. But

all it does is make
him crosser than
I thought was
possible.
Before I
know it, he's
grabbed hold
of me and
flipped me
upside down,
holding me
by the ankles
and shaking me
like a moneybox.

"I want my money back!"

"But you haven't paid me yet!"

"Then I want compensation."

"For what?"

"Damages. To my reputation, and cos someone has to put this mess straight."

And he carries on shaking me. Endlessly. Till

my pockets give in and spit twenty-nine pound coins all over the pavement.

That's his cue to drop me and scoop up a handful of my wages. At least a tenner's worth, I reckon.

"That should cover it," he says. "And I'd suggest you think about a different career. Come within a mile of me with a pair of scissors again and I'll rearrange your face."

And with that he departs, pulling a beanie from his pocket to hide his shame.

I feel myself deflate, but also feel relief flow over me too. Clutching my face, it feels like my nose is still where it was earlier, and so is everything else, and I have to be pleased with that.

I'm also eighteen pounds richer than I was this morning, so it's not all wrecked.

Quickly, I scamper around and scoop the coins back into my pocket, only to be tapped on the shoulder by a rosy-cheeked Giraffles.

"Did you finish Tubs already?"

"Not exactly."

"I found the scissors."

"I think I'm retiring from the barber business."

"Already?"

"Yeah, not sure I'm cut out for it."

I didn't mean it to be funny, but for once Giraffles thinks I'm hilarious.

"So what are you going to do now? To pay for the trip?"

I'm about to shrug, clean out of ideas, when I see a woman walking a dog.

In fact she's not walking a dog. She's walking *eight* of them.

And my ears prick up quicker than a bloodhound's.

Bingo.

Brilliant.

I'm back in the game.

9

Ten minutes into my first ride and we're going so
fast I think we might be in danger of taking off.

It is, without doubt, the most exciting husky
ride of my life.

Kind of.

Because I'm not stood on a sled, I'm stood on
Dyl's old micro-scooter, and it's not *being* pulled
by a pack of highly trained huskies, it's being
dragged by nine different dogs: a Dalmatian,
a Staffie, a Whippet and a host of others that I
know nothing about, other than that they are fast!

What I do know is that if they keep this up, or rather if their owners keep on paying me, I'll have the money in no time. In fact, I'll probably be rich enough to retire!

I grin wildly as the pack pulls me round the park. I still can't believe how easy it was to find so many punters. All I had to do was get up super early and pounce on people as they set off, bleary-eyed for their morning walk. Nobody likes scooping up dog poo at six-thirty in the morning.

Nor do they like traipsing the streets when it's honking down with rain. Not when they could be sat on the sofa with a steaming cup of tea and Netflix on the telly.

Which was pretty much my sales pitch to be honest...

"Wouldn't you rather *me* get cold walking Bonzo instead of you? I'll pick up his poo for you this morning if you like? As many as he can coil out, and it'll only cost you four quid an hour."

They bit my hand off quicker than an Alsatian

that hasn't eaten in a week.

And as for the poo picking?

I haven't scooped up a single one yet. No need, because I've invented this brilliant new game called Poo Golf.

All you need to join in the fun is a stick and a poo, preferably belonging to a dog.

As soon as Fido does his business you take your stick and flick the poo into the nearest bush in as few shots as possible. You get extra points if you can flick the poo into the bush without it

breaking into pieces. Or hitting your shoe by accident.

It's funny the games you can make up at 6.37 in the morning... I give it ten years before you see it in the Olympics.

Anyway, it's worked out a treat, though it's took me a day of having my arms pulled out of their sockets to realize that I needed a vehicle, both to exercise the dogs properly, and to give me the best rush possible.

After three hours of endless searching, I found Dyl's scooter hidden under all his army clobber. And honest, you could've abseiled from Mars to earth with the amount of rope he has stashed away. So I borrowed a bit of that too, building a harness that keeps the dogs safe while they pull me along like Usain Bolt on a superbike.

Which brings me here, beaming at joggers as I hare past them.

And it makes me feel magic, all the speed. Makes me hungry to get to Wild Out and beat every challenge they put in front of me.

BOULDERING? No problem, I'll make 'em look like pebbles.

RAPIDS? Pah, they don't look so quick to me... Right now, with the wind whipping at my face and the G-force blowing my cheeks behind my ears, I feel powerful. For the first time in forty-eight hours, the thought of being shaken upside down by big Tubs doesn't fill me with dread and fear. Not any more.

I feel like I could stand up to him, or Dyl, or any other meathead who comes my way.

No one can touch me. I'm Danny Mack! Prince of Speed, King of the Jungle.

Except, while I'm having these thoughts of grandeur, a cat crosses the path. And my crown most definitely slips...

At first, I don't think the moggy's even going to move. It just stands there, eyes wide, back arched. The dogs, of course, go mental, turning the sled into a fighter jet, but that doesn't bother

67

the cat, which simply hisses like a kettle then roars like a panther, before turning on its tail and legging it.

But the pack howl in reply and tear after it, paying little attention to the highway code or the fact that the cat has left the path and is now haring down the gravel that leads to the skate park.

I feel the surface change under my feet, the vibrations shaking every muscle and cell in my body. I try to adapt – bend my knees, absorb as much of the track as I can – but it's tough, unforgiving, and I see my knuckles turn red, then white, as I cling to the bars of the scooter.

"WHOOOOOOOOOOOOA!" I yelp, trying to remember the names of the dogs and failing miserably, but if anything they take my plea as encouragement and hammer on even quicker, desperate to close the gap between their prey and their jaws.

The gap between the two shortens slightly, and I do my best to steer the scooter clear of potholes and puddles. The wheels respond, somehow, and I start to feel something I don't expect: a tiny, teeny bit of control, and in return a drip-drip-drip of excitement.

I'm doing it.

I'm rolling with the punches, taking everything the dumb cat can throw at me and surfing right over the top of it.

Except then, right then, it's like the cat is listening to my thoughts and thinking, *OK, Danny Mack, let's see what you do with this*, before taking a sharp left towards the skate park.

"OH. MAAAAAAAAN." I yell, as I know only too well what is lying ahead: the most extreme array of bumps, jumps and half-pipes imaginable. The sort of challenges that test the most able of skaters, never mind undersized idiots in charge of nine dogs and a battered microscooter.

The cat is going mental now, dashing in every direction, to avoid not only my trusty pack, but the astonished mob of skaters, who quickly start filming my every move.

They whoop as I grab some serious air off the first ramp, yell as I soar even higher off the second, then cover their eyes (but not their phones) as I head straight down into the half pipe.

I can't begin to explain how it feels as I hit the top of the ramp and follow the dogs skywards. A little bit excited and a lot-a-bit scared: I think at some point I do actually let out a bit of wee in both fear and joy.

Is this how Father Christmas feels, I wonder, when Rudolph and the others pull him into the clouds?

Either way, it's not Christmas Eve, not by a long chalk. And anyway, even Father Christmas has rough landings sometimes, which is exactly what happens to me.

I've ridden my luck for as long as I can, but finally that luck gives way and the board flicks from under my feet, and tears at my fists, ripping them away from the handles.

Onwards the dogs and the scooter fly, still in the direction of the poor, but deeply annoying, cat that I swear is now laughing at me.

And as for me, I go in the only direction available: down.

Down, down, down, until a grass verge reaches up and gives me the biggest and roughest hug of my life.

Ouch.

Ouch. Ouch. Ouch.

10

I wake up with an all-over body tattoo in the shape of a bruise.

It hurts and it stings – but only when I try to move any part of my body, including my eyelids.

But at the same time, I have never been so happy in my life, because on my bedside table is the biggest pile of coins I have ever seen.

In my head, it looks like a million quid, but at the same time I know that it's actually one hundred pounds. On the dot.

Most of it is pound coins, shining like a pile

of pirate's treasure, but there's fifty, twenty, ten, five, two and even one pence pieces, which makes me really, really happy 'cos it reminds me that I earned every single penny myself.

The pain doesn't hurt half as much, though, when you've proved a point to yourself, and so I manage to have a shower and try (unsuccessfully) to tame my hair. I smile when my mum gives me a hug and hands over the final fifty quid, though I also feel a bit guilty about taking it off her. Maybe if I'd worked a bit harder, I could've raised the whole amount myself.

I have to walk to school slowly – a result of the bruise tattoo and the fact that I'm carrying two tons of loose change in my pockets – but that only gives me more time to become even more excited about the trip.

"What are you looking forward to most?" I ask the rest of the crew.

"Bouldering," reply MandM in unison, without pause or consultation.

"Kayaking," says Giraffles, and I momentarily wonder if they'll have to make a special one to fit his epically long limbs.

Lucky takes his time before shouting the most perfect sentence imaginable:

"ALL OF IT!"

I'd jump on his back in wild agreement if my legs weren't so heavy with coins, because he's nailed it. That's EXACTLY what I'm thinking. This is going to be the most perfectest trip known to man. Or woman. Or child.

And that is what I'm thinking as we walk into the playground. I'm even still thinking it when I hear someone shout my name in a tone that can only be described as vicious.

"Are you Danny Mack?" It belongs to a woman with a perm as angry and wound up as her accusation.

"Er..." my hesitation kind of gives me away, and the woman drags a small, cowering boy out from behind her legs. A boy with a haircut so disastrous that there can only be one explanation for it. That I was his hairdresser.

"I need a word with you," she says, before continuing to shout loads of them at me. "What did you do to our Cameron? He used to have lovely hair. Like a little prince he was. But now? Well, thanks to you he looks like a bloomin' orc."

I don't know what to say, so I say the wrong thing, obviously.

"But that's the look we were going for. He told me his favourite book was *Lord of the Rings*, and let's face it, no one wants a Hobbit cut. They're *so* last year."

In my head it's funny, or at least witty, but to the woman standing before me it's the final insult she's been waiting for, and just like Tubs, she threatens to turn me upside down until she gets her money back.

I save her the trouble, and me the pain and shame, by digging four quid out of my pocket, though it isn't until I let go of the money that I realize what it means.

That I only have one hundred and forty-six quid. And to go on the trip, I need one hundred and fifty. I feel myself sag, and my bruises start shouting a whole lot louder.

Thirty seconds later and they're screaming, when another livid mother does exactly the same thing, so I rush to the door only to be collared a third flipping time, which leads to another refund. By the time I make it to class my pockets are lighter.

Twelve quid lighter.

And the money is due in T-minus ninety seconds. Now, I'm a quick thinker, but even I'm stumped. What can I do? Beg for more time? Beg Mum for more? I can't do either, as Miss made it clear that today is the absolute deadline with no exceptions.

So I slump to my seat, allowing my head to whack on to the desktop, where I intend to leave it until 3.15 p.m.

"OK everybody, good morning," sings Miss D

from the front. "So, who has trip money for me?"

I watch a trail of classmates wind their way to the front, fist-bumping and grinning as they sign up to the single greatest activity ever. I push my forehead even harder on to the desktop.

"Danny?" Miss D is calling me now. "Danny, have you got yours, love?"

I don't know what to say. I can't say it out loud, cos it's like admitting I'm a complete pauper in front of everyone I know, so, with pockets jangling, I slump to her desk.

"Come on, sunshine. Hand it over. I know how hard you've been working for this."

"I've decided not to go, Miss," I say, quietly. "Not sure it's for me." Forcing out the lie hurts way more than any bruise in the world.

Her eyes widen and her jaw goes limp. "But you've been walking all those dogs."

I feel the tears gather behind my eyes, and I know she sees it.

"What is it, Danny? You can tell me."

"I can't afford it, Miss. I thought I could, but I can't."

She sighs, and peers over my shoulder at the rest of the class before lowering her voice as she says, "Do you have your money with you?"

I nod.

"Then pass it over and let me count it. Perhaps you've just totted it up wrong."

I tell her I haven't, but she insists, so I pile the coins up on her desk like a molehill, and she tells us all to get on with silent reading for ten minutes.

So we do as she says – well, the others do. I pretend to read while watching her move the money into piles, then see her frown and sigh as she too realizes that I'm twelve quid short.

I want to look away then, out of shame, but for some reason I don't, and instead I see Miss reach under her desk and into her bag, where she rummages for a few seconds.

Then, with the deftest of hands, she palms a note and two coins besides my pile, before lifting her head and smiling.

"Oh, Danny, you soft lad," she grins. "We really do need to work on your addition, don't we? It's all here. A hundred and fifty pounds. Perfect."

I don't know what to say. I know what she's done, and it's just about the best and kindest thing anyone could ever do for me (except perhaps teaching me to cut hair properly). I spend the next hour till playtime trying not to get all cry-y about it.

So when the bell rings and the others file out, I pretend to tie my laces, until there's only me and Miss D left in the room.

"I know what you did," I tell her. "And I don't know what to say, except thank you."

She smiles. "I have no idea what you're talking about, Daniel Mack."

She's embarrassed now and I don't want to make it worse. So I simply say, "I'll pay you back, Miss. Promise I will," and walk on.

And as I reach the door, I hear her faintly reply, "I know you will, son. I know."

Off into the yard I go, to find something to jump off.

If I'm going to do this properly, then I'm going to need all the practice I can get.

There is no way I am missing the bus.

I know this because I am an hour early for it. In fact, when I arrive I'm the first person in the playground, apart from the fox that's rifling through the bins.

Mum gets a bit teary when I say goodbye, unlike Dyl who doesn't even surface from his coffin of a bedroom. Mum makes up for it by pulling me into a bear hug that would surely suffocate a lesser man than me. Then the phone rings, which allows me to escape before she can do any actual damage.

I don't feel the weight of my rucksack, even though it's holding just about every item of clothing I own. There were loads of things that I didn't have. I mean, who has walking boots when they only ever set foot on tarmac?

And as for a head torch: have they never heard of streetlights? Or phones?

Anyway, the minutes pass, the excitement builds and so does the number of us waiting in the yard.

Giraffles pitches up with a lump of a rucksack on his back that makes him look like more of a camel than a giraffe, MandM arrive in matching everything, while Lucky makes the biggest entrance. Literally everything he's wearing or carrying is brand new and top of the range, though he doesn't make a fuss about it. If anything, he looks slightly embarrassed by it all. With a bit of luck, he might have some spare stuff that I can borrow...

There's a cheer and a Mexican wave when the

coach arrives, then a scrum as we pile on, fighting to get to the back seats, as far away from the bog as possible, though we've already been warned that it's a "pee-only facility" by the driver.

Anyone attempting anything else will be "hung, drawn and tortured", then "tarred and feathered." We all smile politely as the driver issues the threats, but to be honest I don't think any of us have a clue what he's banging on about.

Instead, we sit there excitedly, and break open our packed lunches for the good stuff in there, but then … nothing happens. We go nowhere. And out on the playground there's a cluster of teachers scratching their chins and checking their watches. We know something's going on, and it can't be good cos they're not saying a word to us. So when Miss D gets on, looking unusually flustered, I ask if there's anything wrong.

"Well, we are running a little bit late, as one of the adults due to be coming to help has twisted her ankle, and without another responsible person

to come and supervise, I'm afraid we wouldn't be able to go."

There's an enormous groan of disappointment, but I'm not feeling it. No way. I'm not disappointed; I'm *freaking out*. What if we can't go? After all the hard work and bruises and near-death experiences? Are you kidding me?

It throws me so badly I think I'm going to be sick, and I wonder what the driver would do to me if I threw up in his wee-only lav? But just as I start searching for a paper bag to breathe into, Miss D chirps up with the punchline.

"But it's all fine now. We've found, at the last minute, a replacement helper."

I punch the air, narrowly missing Giraffles by accident.

"Now it's not another teacher, but I want all of you to act respectfully to our volunteer, just as you would anyone else."

There's an unusual force in her voice, and she seems to be looking at me a lot as she says it, with a strange expression on her face that seems to change from apologetic to forceful and back again, as if on rotation.

I don't get it. Why is she singling me out? I've never had a detention in my life. If I wasn't so stoked at the fact that the trip's back on, I might even be a bit offended.

"Now some of you will know our knight in shining armour, so please can you give him a huge round of applause?"

Clapping fills the bus, and I join in – 'course I do. But only momentarily, as our saviour appears between the front seats.

And let me tell you, this is no knight.

It's a rat.

A lousy, stinking rat that's going to ruin my fun.

And his name ... is Dylan.

12

Older brothers are put on this planet for one reason: to make life a living hell.

All my life Dylan's been doing that. I swear, my earliest memory is of him leaning over my cot and rubbing his hands together before nicking the dummy from my mouth.

Since then, he's kicked me and punched me, drawn on me when I'm asleep and told me I was the world's first living brain donor.

He's done everything in his power to make me his victim, and look at what he's done now:

hijacked the one thing that I thought I might get some joy out of.

I'd write down a rude word for him right now, but he'd probably find a way of ruining that for me too. Make my pen squirt ink in my face or something.

Instead, I ignore him for the entire journey, despite the fact that I can feel him looking at me and hear him laughing.

Miss D does come to talk to me though, pulling me aside to tell me what happened.

"I can see that you're not very happy about this situation, Danny."

I shrug, which takes some restraint, as I actually want to scream **"THIS IS MY WORST NIGHTMARE BROUGHT TO LIFE!!!"**

"I know how much this trip means to you. More than anyone else in the whole class. And I know that your relationship with your brother isn't always the best…"

I raise my eyebrow so high it almost hits the roof of the coach.

"...But believe me, Danny, I had no choice. It was Dylan or no trip. No one else could come at such short notice, and we needed a responsible adult to help out."

"Responsible? *Dyl?*" The words catch in my throat like I've tried to swallow a killer whale in one gulp. "He can't even spell the word, and he DEFINITELY doesn't know what it means. He puts pepper on my cornflakes and worms in my bed. He has the intellect of a mashed potato. I wouldn't put him in charge of a sunflower seed, never mind thirty of us!"

Miss does everything I expect of her. She smiles sadly and nods. It's like she can actually feel my pain. It's like she actually agrees with me. But then she also says this:

"He's sixteen years old, Danny. Which means he can help us. I promise I will not let him spoil your trip. You have my word."

I plaster a smile on my face and thank her. But she doesn't know Dyl like I do. He's slyer than a fox. I stare out of the window, trying to pre-empt every bit of torture heading my way.

The next four hours drag by. Well, they do until we get out of the city, which is slow and painful work. I could walk quicker on my hands than our bus moves for the first ninety minutes. In fact, it takes so long I expect it to get dark by the time we reach the countryside. But it doesn't. If anything, it gets lighter, and after staring confusedly for a while, I work out why: there's no tower blocks blocking out the sun. No huge ad boards or phone masts either, just the occasional looming pylon.

It's weird, like I've just landed on the moon or something. It looks alien. And even though I'm safely tucked inside a comfy bus, with a "pee-only" bog, I feel a bit weird too. Like I'm a long way from home. Like the rules outside are different to the ones I'm used to. The cars move quicker here. There are fewer traffic lights. And there's way less people, but more animals.

It seems like I'm not the only one feeling the change either. There's a kid in our class called Jonny Walker. He's all right, harmless enough, but for the last two years I don't think I've ever seen him with his head out of his phone. Until today, cos Miss D has banned all screens until tonight, so poor Jonny is watching the world go by, his head twisting backwards and forwards so quickly it's like he's watching a game of tennis on fast forward.

Anyway, about two hours in, Jonny spots a bunch of animals in the distance, grazing in a field, and I swear to you, no word of a lie, he shouts:

"Look! Rhinos!"

And like a bunch of idiots we all spin round, to see ... not rhinos, but cows.

It is, without doubt, the stupidest thing I have ever heard in my life, but for a minute, a split second, we all think it's true.

Jonny blushes when he's called out on it. I'm pretty sure one of the cows even shakes his head as we sail past.

"*What*?!" says Jonny with a shrug. "Anyone could've made the same mistake. It's not like I've ever seen one before."

And that makes me think, cos you know what? It's the same for me – for most of us, probably. Foxes, yes, rats occasionally. But cows? That weren't on a TV screen?

Nope.

So I do what I can to make him feel better "Easy mistake to make," I say. "We've got a Giraffles *inside* the bus, so why not a rhino out there?"

And he laughs, and so does old Giraffles, and you know what? For a while I stop thinking about our Dylan, who's still staring out the window, probably mistaking the cow for a Stegosaurus.

Once, we get there, I think to myself, it'll be fine.

And I think it so hard that it rolls around in my head on a loop, even when I manage to fall asleep against the window.

13

I wake with a start, Dyl screaming in my ear.

"FIRE!" he yells. **"SAVE YOURSELF! WOMEN, CHILDREN AND IDIOT BROTHERS FIRST!"**

I know I shouldn't buy it. I've known him all my life, witnessed his wind-ups every day of my freaking existence, but I was properly asleep when he did it - dribbling, and dreaming about abseiling the world's biggest mountain. (Somehow I managed to do it without any kind of rope, like Bear Grylls crossed with Dumbledore.) So when

Dyl sounds the foghorn in my lughole I jump instinctively on to my seat, cracking my head on the luggage rack above.

I crumple, half of my brain probably clinging to the rack still, and Dyl brays like a donkey, slapping Giraffles and MandM on the arms, reminding them of just how hilarious he is.

But as they've met him before, they actually know what a dufus he is, and turn instead to help me up.

"C'mon," says Marcus.

"We're here," says Maureen, which cheers me up no end.

Even Miss D isn't impressed with Dyl, fixing him with a look so sour it could turn milk to cheese in seconds.

I stumble from the bus, rubbing my bonce, taking in a couple of HUGE mountains in the distance, my ears hearing something that has to be a river. It gets my pulse racing, dreaming about the excitement that lies ahead.

But right outside the bus, there's not really a lot to see.

Perhaps I was expecting log cabins, or shacks at least, with little chimneys pumping smoke from them. Maybe I thought we'd be greeted by a team of buff-looking outdoorsy types too, but neither of these things are *anywhere* in sight. All I *can* see is a huge pile of long canvas bags and a woman stood beside them, who at first sight appears to be around one hundred and thirty two years old. She's not stooped over or anything, far from it, she's stood bolt upright, almost like she's on parade, but her face is crumpled like a ball of paper, her hair as thin as spiders' webs, and her arms ... well, they wouldn't look out of place on a snowman.

The second she opens her mouth though, we know who's in charge.

"MY FRIENDS!" she booms, the force of her voice blowing us all back a pace or two. **"WELCOME TO WILD OUT!"** She has an accent that is impossible to place, though it is most definitely posh. Posh but properly, properly friendly.

"My name is Geraldine Farquaharson-Smythe, though my friends and recruits," and she points at us in turn, "call me Geri. I am the founder of this wonderful establishment." Again, she points a skeletal finger, this time at the field that surrounds us.

We turn as one, looking for what she's pointing at. Unless all the buildings are really well camouflaged, there is literally nothing to see.

"I wish I could explain to you fully about the delights that are heading your way. I wish I could

98

tell you fully about the perilous climbing, and mind-bending orienteering. I wish you could picture the river kayaking or zip-lining, but I don't have the words. All I can do is insist that you savour every moment that comes your way. It will test you physically and mentally, but you WILL never forget it, you have my word! Now, you must be exhausted after such a long and arduous journey, but, worry not, I have a feast fit for the hungriest platoon waiting for you, just as soon as you build your accommodation. So, my new recruits, bend your backs, get stuck in, and soon you will be eating nothing but the freshest and finest cuisine we can offer."

Giraffles looks confused "I didn't see a McDonalds on the way in, did you?" he whispers.

I shake my head. "There's probably a drive-in disguised as a tree or something," I say. Though, to be honest, I'm more confused about how the canvas sacks in front of us are possibly going to turn into a hotel.

Unlike the others, I have the sense to keep my mouth shut…

"Er … Miss?" asks Hannah Sycamore. "Are we sleeping on the bus or something?"

But before Miss D can answer, Geri shakes her head and points a bony finger at the canvas sacks.

"What? The hotel's underground?" asks Rosie Sim, sparing Hannah's blushes but causing a rainbow of her own.

"No, *no*, my dear old thing," booms Geri. "Tents! In the bag there. Each tent sleeps three. So get stuck in. Last one to get theirs up is a rotten egg! And besides…" She stops, raises her head to the clouds and sniffs, long and hard… "There's a storm brewing."

Our eyes narrow in confusion, and I look up and sniff too, but only get a whiff of our Dylan, who hasn't showered in the last six months.

"Best do as she says," I whisper to Giraffles, and we grab Lucky to share with us, because we know he's bound to have the best snacks in his bag, plus there is NO WAY I am sharing with Dyl and his toxic feet.

We haul a bag from the pile, pull it to a flat piece of field, and tip its contents at our feet, frowning at the endless poles, ropes and canvas sheets that sit there.

"Where's the instructions?" I ask sensibly.

Giraffles searches, almost climbing inside the sack and wearing it as a balaclava before muffledly shouting, "There aren't any."

"Indeed there aren't," confirms Geri, appearing at our shoulders. "Missions don't come with a manual. So fire up your initiative and engage your instincts!"

She marches on, and we hear a whirring as she walks.

"Do you think that's her hearing aid making that noise?" I ask Lucky.

"Nah, more likely it's her electric hip."

Giraffles giggles. "It's not just her hip that's metallic. That Geri's not human. She can't be at her age. She's a cyborg and that's her brain you

101

can hear. Her brain and her titanium skeleton."

I weigh up Giraffles' theory as I watch her strut to the next group. Seems unlikely, I think, but I'm not going to rule anything out.

"We don't need instructions anyway," laughs Lucky, "Cos look who's got Google and unlimited data right here." He whips out a phone so swanky it looks like it belongs in a Star Wars movie.

His fingers flash across the screen, but the phone is not as speedy. In fact, nothing happens. The screen simply turns blank, apart from two words.

Two words that strike fear into city kids like us.

No signal.

Lucky turns pale, and looks at us with dread in his eyes.

"I don't like this, lads," he says with a shiver. "I think I want to go home."

The news spreads like wildfire.

There are wide eyes and slack jaws.

There are cries of dismay and a wave of phones being pulled from pockets because no one believes the rumours are true.

Jonny Walker actually falls to his knees and howls at the moon, which seems a bit over the top to be honest, but I'm more concerned with working out what this mess of poles and canvas actually turns into. Plus, the light is starting to fail and old Geri doesn't look like the sort to bail you out just because it's getting dark and that's when the grizzly bears come out to play.

We make a start. Well, we do after we've looked at what everyone else is doing and we can copy them.

I even look to see how Dyl has tackled it, which makes me feel a bit sick inside. For some strange reason he has a three-man tent all to himself, but even without any help his tent is already upright and he's hammering in the pegs and guy ropes. He looks proper smug about it as well, standing to attention as Geri approaches and snapping out a salute. I decide to check with Mum when I get home to see if he was actually adopted.

"No need to salute, soldier," Geri barks. "You're not in the services yet."

"Won't be long though, ma'am." Dyl doesn't let his salute drop, so Geri offers him a hand to shake instead.

"Well let's see what you're made of these next few days, eh?" and she closes her fist around his.

The result is slow at first but builds quickly, like when you eat a red chilli by mistake and your mouth gradually feels like it's been set fire to. I see it in Dyl's eyes. They narrow in confusion, then slowly, slowly widen as he realizes he's actually shaking hands with something resembling a boa constrictor.

I don't know if Geri's doing it because she's seen through our Dyl already, or just because she likes to test the strongest recruits, but she squeezes harder. And harder. And harder still, until it looks like Dyl is having trouble breathing. His fingertips have turned the purest white, but his face is kind of blue, and I'm imagining that his brain is racing, trying to work out how he's been taken down by a pensioner from the Iron Age.

"Can you hear that?" whispers Giraffles. "Her hand, it's whirring again… I swear that Geri is pure robot."

"Then let's get this bloomin' tent up before she tries to shake anything that's attached to our bodies."

So we try. Really we do, for what seems like hours. And we do manage to make some things, but *none* of them are tents.

We create a canoe (kind of), a 1975 Volkswagen Beetle (if you use your imagination), and if you screw your eyes up really tight we seem to create a life-size version of the Statue of Liberty.

But seeing as none of them are a tent, and none of them use every single piece of kit in the bag, we realize we've not quite got it right and have to start over again.

Finally, after much wailing, arguing and innocent cheating by inspecting everyone else's efforts, we have something that resembles a tent. There's still one spare pole left (annoyingly), but we pretend it never existed and ram it back inside the bag.

"I'm going in," says Giraffles excitedly, and folds his long limbs inside, only to start banging the sides of the tent repeatedly, like he's trying to swat a particularly annoying fly.

"What are you doing?" I yell.

"I'm looking for the light switch," he replies. "It's well dark in here!"

I laugh. I laugh like I've never laughed before, not even that time when Dyl tried to wash his legs in the toilet then got stuck when he accidentally flushed it. And what makes it even better is that Lucky is as confused as Giraffles.

"You're kidding me?" he yells. "It must be in there." And he dives in too, with much thrashing and confusion.

"Never mind the light switch," Lucky shouts, "I

107

can't find the electric socket either, or the wifi box."

"And where are the beds?" adds Giraffles, just as Geri approaches. She smiles, but shakes her head.

"I think they might be in for a shock," she says to me.

"Don't think they've ever slept in a tent," I reply.

"And what about you, Danny?"

"Oh yeah," I lie. "All the time."

She stares at me, hard. And I swear I hear a whirring as her eyeballs narrow, like they're drilling into my brain, searching for the truth.

"I'd, er… I'd better explain to them what a sleeping bag is," I stammer. Though to be honest, I'm not exactly sure either.

I'm not sure about much any more. But I'm sure it'll all seem better in the morning…

15

I woke up super early.

So early I never actually went to sleep – how could I when the countryside is so flipping noisy?

All night there were grunts and groans and snuffles and wails, but only 37% of those came from inside the tent (though some of those noises smelt rank).

I have no idea what was prowling around outside, but I'm glad Jonny Walker wasn't in our tent, cos in his head it was probably a T-Rex and a raptor having a disco.

Got to admit, though, that by three a.m. my sleep-wrecked imagination was going a bit mental too. I'm sure at some point I heard Dylan out there, wrestling with whatever was on the prowl, and I felt relief in the fact that the stegosaurus was probably going to rip him limb from limb.

"Euuuurghhhhhh," comes a noise from Lucky's sleeping bag, and for once it doesn't seem to be coming from his backside. "I have not slept a wink all night."

"Your bum's been wide awake, believe me," I reply.

"It's this mattress, Dan, it's like sleeping on a digestive biscuit."

My tummy rumbles at the mention of food. We'd all been too tired to do anything but crawl inside our tents when we'd finished, and although Lucky had sweets aplenty in his bag, there weren't enough to stop me being as hungry as I was tired.

So after wrestling with the zip for what feels like an eternity, I fall out of the tent to be confronted with a legion of the roughest-looking zombies imaginable, who are, in fact, just my classmates who have had as little sleep as me.

Many of them don't have bags under their eyes as much as suitcases, while poor Jonny Walker is on his knees, weeping on to his mobile phone.

"I just don't understand," he wails. "How can there be no signal…?"

It's not a conversation I want to get involved with, so I give him a wide steer, and instead accidentally fall into the clutches of Dyl, who is doing chin-ups from a tree so old that it looks like it was planted when a caveman spat out an acorn because of a nut allergy.

Dylan greeted me in a typical way.

"Sleep well, loser?"

"Thought you were exercising your body, not your tiny mind," I reply, well used to our morning routine.

"This beautiful body has already run ten kilometres this morning. What exercise have you done?"

I think about telling him had survived a deadly gas attack, thanks to Lucky's rotten guts, but I'm so hungry I stop myself and head instead to the others, who are grouped around a long, thin table, with tree trunks for chairs.

"What's for breakfast?" I ask, as there's no sign of any Coco Pops. Or a Weetabix. Not even a crunchy nut flake. Just a pile of spoons, bowls, and a load of old tin buckets.

We don't have long to wait though, as Geri shouts from behind us.

"My lovely recruits … breakfast is served!"

We spin around, hopeful for cereal, toast or even some fruit if we have to, but – no, oh no – Geri is walking towards us flanked by a couple of the BIGGEST beasts I have ever seen.

"COWS?" I yell, before Jonny shouts rhino or tiger or something equally stupid.

They're scary somehow. How did they get so wide? And one of them is pure white (apart from random dark splodges that I can only guess are

poo), while the other is dark, dark brown. "We're having burgers?" says Giraffles. "For breakfast?" "Don't be ridiculous," replies Marcus, before Maureen adds, "Burgers aren't made of cows. They're made of meat."

"Yeah, but the meat has got to come from somewhere, so where does it come from, eh?"

Neither M nor M has an answer to that, though Jonny tries to find out the answer on his phone before he gets yet another painful reminder of the signal problem.

Thankfully, old Geri comes to the rescue. "You all make an excellent point: too often we eat and drink things without a clue about where the food comes from. Well, not today! In fact, not while you are here at all. Burgers DO often come from cows" – at this, MandM look on the verge of passing out in shock – "but we will not be eating Flossy and Rossy here, we will simply be milking them. Or at least, you will."

"For what?" asks Jonny, with a completely straight face, which even shocks Geri.

"Well, for the milk."

"Oh," grins Jonny, like the penny has finally dropped. He pauses, nods, then adds:

"So where's the pink one then?"

"The pink what?"

"The pink cow."

Geri looks well confused, and, for the first time, a bit irritated. "Why would we have a pink cow?"

Now it's Jonny's turn now to look at her like

she's daft. "Well, it's obvious innit? The white cow is vanilla, the brown one gives chocolate. So where's the pink cow, cos I'd like a strawberry milkshake?"

Jonny stops talking and there's silence. Deafening, tumbleweed silence.

And then laughter.

Loads of it.

So much laughter that poor old plonker Jonny turns redder than a scarlet cow. So red that I almost wish he was a cow, so we could have the finest raspberry milkshake the world has ever tasted.

16

Never in my life will I ever again walk past
a supermarket without running up to it and
hugging it like it was my mum.

For the past two hours I would have snogged
a corner shop, never mind a full-size one. I can
see their fridges now, with more milk than you
can imagine: red top, green top, blue top. Heck,
right now I am SO HUNGRY I would even drink
almond milk (whatever that is).

It's been ridiculous, emotional, tiring. I don't
know how I thought farmers got milk out of cows

– I'm sure they've got machines that help, but Geri wasn't having any of that.

"The only machines you need are these things," she says, as she wiggles her arthritic fingers before showing us how to use them as pumps on the cows' udders. Cue much yelling of:

"EUGH!"
"GROSS!"
"I AM NOT TOUCHING THAT!"

But I don't mind, and anyway the milk pours out at such a rate when she touches them that I'm convinced there's actually a hidden tap she's turned to get it flowing.

"I'll have a go," I say, when she asks for volunteers, and I sit at this weird three-legged stool that she places next to Flossy (or is it Rossy? It doesn't really matter either way).

"Now don't be shy," she says. "Their udders aren't as sensitive as they look, so you can afford to grip tightly."

I do as she says, flinching as my hands wrap round what look like an over-inflated rubber glove. With every muscle in my body tense, and my eyes welded shut in a grimace, I pull, and…

Nothing.

I pull again. Harder.

Still nothing.

So I try once more, though I presume I may have been a little too rough, as the cow bucks like a rodeo horse, kicking the steel bucket with more force than a Ronaldo free kick so it narrowly misses the right of Dyl's head.

"Do that again and you're flipping dead!"

he hisses, and I make a note to pull slightly
to the left next time. Well, I would if I wasn't
traumatized by what just happened.

"Let's give someone else a go, shall we?" smiles
Geri through gritted teeth. But everyone else is
just as bad as me.

Giraffles can't tease out a drop, and neither
can MandM, despite milking Flossy and Rossy
at the same flipping time. Jonny is rubbish at it,
probably because he's holding his phone at the
same time, and even Lucky comes up short. In
fact, his efforts make Rossy empty his guts.

"Good luck putting that on your porridge,"
sneers Dyl, before pushing Lucky aside and
sitting on the stool. "Time to watch a master at
work…" He cracks his knuckles, blows on them,
and wraps his fingers round the udders, moving
with the speed and precision of a concert pianist.

Instantly, we hear a noise. A faint tinkling,
which reminds us with a thump to the head just
how bloomin' hungry we are. We bend down to see

a thin jet of liquid hitting the inside of the bucket.

"What is that?!" yells Jonny, like it's the most disgusting thing he has ever seen in his life.

"It's milk, you idiot!" we yell as one, before we break into a weird kind of rain dance. Except it's not a rain dance, it's a milk dance. And I know I shouldn't be celebrating cos it's Dyl who's made it rain after all, but right now I want porridge more than I've ever wanted anything in my life, so as long as he doesn't gloat or milk his success (sorry) too badly, I'm prepared to overlook it.

In fact, his success makes me even more determined to make it work myself, so I grab a stool, park myself beside Rossy, and pull and pump until finally, FINALLY, I get some milk out of her swollen udders.

It's not a torrent. It's barely even a trickle to be honest, but it's my trickle, and I did it without use of Google. And when I taste the porridge that I've made with way too little (but incredibly fresh) milk? I'm telling you, it's the BEST thing I have eaten in my flippin' life. Even when Dyl sneezes in it on purpose, he doesn't spoil it.

I eat it all. You bet I do. Because if this morning is anything to go by, I'm going to need every bit of energy I can get.

17

So I've eaten, kind of. And even though it was
hardly a feast, I'm ready. You know, to climb stuff,
and jump off stuff, or even fall off stuff (which is
way more likely, given my career as a free runner
so far).

But two minutes into packing my rucksack for
the day I feel a rumble that isn't hunger. I need to
… go.

No, not home – no way.

You know … go.

And I realize I have no idea where the loo even

is, but I'd better find out sharpish.

I duck out of the tent, failing to stay on my feet yet again, which doesn't help the fact that I now really need to go.

I see MandM walking towards me, and for some reason it pops into my head to ask them what they do when one of them needs the loo. Surely they separate long enough for that to happen, but does one of them wait outside the bathroom door? Fortunately, another twinge in my belly forces the thought from my head.

"Where's the bog?" I ask, doing the "I need the loo" run, which involves clamping your bum cheeks so firmly closed that you only move from the knees down.

They both point towards them with such certainty that it makes me think maybe they DO go to the loo at the same time, but I shake off that thought and waddle urgently to a small but tall tent at the far end of the field.

It's nothing like any kind of public toilet I've

ever seen before, but I'm that desperate that I push the canvas aside and step straight in, only for my nostrils to be walloped by the most putrid, nose-eating whiff I have ever smelt in my life – and I know what evil smells like: it smells like Dylan.

The tent is tiny, so it only takes me 0.3 of a second to work out what smells, and it's the loo itself. Well, I say the loo. It isn't a loo. It's a bucket. With a bin liner inside and a loo seat balanced precariously on top.

As if that isn't bad enough, there's no flush! Now I'm no snob, I live in a block with, like, a million other people, and some of

those people have questionable hygiene, but I bet you that every single one of those people has a flushable bog, and that they wouldn't share that bog with the rest of their class – and their cave man of a brother – if it didn't flippin' flush.

I tell myself not to look in the bucket.

Don't look don't look don't look don't look…

But then I look, 'course I do, and my stomach flips and lurches and my porridge does the same and I have no option but to turn around and sit down – all without falling off the bucket.

But don't worry, that's where the detail stops, honest, cos I do what I need to do, and feel such a surge of relief that I've been and no one – in particular, me – died.

So I look for the toilet paper, cos the sooner that's done the sooner I can breathe fresh air and delete the memory that this ever even happened.

But the thing is, there is no paper.

Not a piece, a shred, a particle. In fact, in horror I realize that there probably wasn't any to start with cos there's no empty cardboard rolls there either, not even on the floor.

And I start to panic. Wouldn't you? All I want to do is get out of here and climb a bloomin' mountain but I can't, because of the obvious.

So I do what any self-respecting, but slightly panicking eleven year old would do:

I shout for my best friend.

"GIRAAAAAAAAAFLLLEEEEEEEES!!!"

I yell, so loudly that I'm sure a pack of actual giraffes in Africa hear me as well as the human one I was calling.

There's no reply. So I call again. And again. And again. In fact, I call so many times that I'm in danger of losing my voice and I start to fear that I might die of suffocation or toxic shock or something.

I feel like one of them people clinging to an iceberg after the Titanic had gone down, except it's boiling hot in here now and the only way I'm going to drown is in my own sweat.

And then, just when I think all hope is lost, I hear him, like a heavenly angel with a super-long neck.

"Danny? That you in there? You OK?"

"Don't come in!" I gasp, then realize that no one with half a brain cell would even consider it.

"Giraffles, mate. Disaster. There's no loo roll in here."

There's a pause, then, "So what do you wipe your bum on?"

"That's why I'm calling you. What do I do?"

"Well I don't know, do I?"

"Have you got any?"

"Any what?"

"Loo roll, you idiot!"

There's an agonizing pause.

"No … but I have got this," and his hand appears through the canvas slit, holding the mankiest piece of tissue you have ever seen in your life. It looks like it's blown his nose, and everyone else's for that matter, for the last nine-and-half years.

"I can't use that!" I squeal.

"Well that's all I've got."

"Then go and ask Geri for some, will you? Quick! It stinks in here."

I hear him amble away, muttering, "Too much information," as he goes.

And he's gone an age. Or it could actually only be a minute, but it feels like an age, and when he comes back, the news is not good.

"She says she hasn't got any. Says we have to use a dock leaf, whatever that is. Oh, and she also says, whatever you do, don't use a nettle, cos apparently nature often makes them grow next to each other. Fascinating that, eh? I had no idea did y—"

"PLEASE," I squeal, **"PLEASE, FOR THE SAKE OF MY NOSE, GET ME A DOCK LEAF, QUICK! IN FACT, GET ME THREE!"**

I wait again. Eyes stinging, hope fading, mood falling, until finally, FINALLY, a hairy hand appears through the slit, clutching a carrier bag

with a load of
leaves in.

I look inside,
frowning. I've
never seen a dock
leaf in my life, but
these look a bit, I
don't know, spiky...
"Mate, are you sure
these are the right ones?"
I ask.

The hand gives me a thumbs-up.

"Did you check with Geri?"

Two hands appear, both of them giving me a
thumb.

I wonder why he's not talking any more, then
a wave of embarrassment hits me: it must be the
smell. It's obviously killing him, and I feel so
ashamed but also grateful that my mate would do
this for me that I shove my hand into the bag and
instantly thrust the leaves against my bum.

What a relief. I'll be out in seconds... Nearly done. Nearly...

"AAAAAARGHHHHHHHH!"

I don't what starts to sting first, my hand or my bum, in fact, it doesn't even matter. All that matters is that I'm in pain. Red-hot agony. Agony that cannot be ignored. In a second I'm on my feet with the bucket lying on its side, and it's all my fault. Not that I care – all I care about is the fact that my bum (and my hand) is on fire, and unless I find water, quickly, someone is going to have to call Fireman Sam.

Without thinking, I dash from the tent, not knowing, never mind caring, that my trousers are still round my ankles.

I waddle in circles, falling occasionally, squealing repeatedly for WATER!

There are gasps, cries and laughter. And of course, who is laughing loudest?

Not Giraffles, cos he's just appeared out of the

131

trees, looking shocked, clutching a load of leaves so soft they sort of look like they're made of kitten fur.

It's Dylan. Laughing so loud he's bent double, wheezing.

And where is he standing? Right by the toilet tent, him and the hairy hands that passed me the bag in the first place.

I want to hurt him. I want to humiliate him. I want to…

STOP MY BUM FROM BURNING!

So, as much as it pains me, I ignore my toe-rag of a brother, and go running in the direction of Miss D, who by now, seems to be trembling. And covering her eyes.

18

By late afternoon, day two of the single greatest trip of my life, the only thing that is going wild is … my bottom.

Actually, that's not true. Every other kid in my class, plus my demonic cretin of a brother, is going wild right this second, climbing a rock face. The torture starts as I lie in the tent, ice pack on bum, forced to listen as Geri talks about the day ahead.

"Recruits. It may be day one, but my word this is no easy introduction. Rock climbing demands so much. Strength, stamina and a sharp, analytical mind. And believe me, you will need all of this if you are to conquer the rock I'm going to put in front of you. It will be tough. Your body and your brain will ache by the end, but the views from the top will make it all worthwhile, believe me."

These are hardly words to cheer me up, and it's made worse when I hear them excitedly gathering their stuff. Giraffles and Lucky look sheepish when they pop back into the tent for their rucksacks.

Strangely enough, neither of them volunteer to stay behind with me. Not that I blame them.

But this is nothing compared to the torture that follows. Hours and hours of hearing them whoop and yell and laugh.

I can hear it despite burying my head below every sleeping bag, roll mat and pillow that I can find in our tent.

"Stupid tent…" I moan. "Stupid tent with their stupid flimsy walls that aren't even walls cos they're not even made out of bricks…"

It's fair to say that I might be feeling a teensy bit sorry for myself, but you would too if you were me. I mean, when was the last time you had to tell your favourite teacher and a retired female sergeant major that you're in agony cos you just wiped your bum with a load of nettles?

When was the last time you were in flippin' agony and in fear of having your bum amputated, yet daren't let any of the staff inspect the damage cos you'd die of embarrassment if they did?

And when was the last time your older brother told all your mates that you've done it on purpose, not just to get sympathy but also because you've got a rare brain disease that makes you addicted to bum pain?

Not lately I'd imagine, so forgive me if I'm a teeny tiny bit upset.

All I can do is lie here, without moving a muscle – especially a bum muscle – cos if I do, the ice pack balanced on my injuries falls off and I have to shout for help to get it placed securely on the cheeks again. Oh yeah, this really is the gift that keeps on giving…

So I lie here, thinking of ways of getting my revenge that don't involve:

A. Killing Dyl stone dead

B. Going to prison, and/or

C. Upsetting Mum

Whilst at the same time causing Dyl the maximum amounts of both physical and mental pain. But as it turns out, I'm not that good at revenge – certainly nowhere near as good as him, anyway. As soon as I let my imagination go, it gets grisly and he ends up being ripped to shreds by a rhino that I hire from a local safari park, which leads straight to point A coming true, followed by B and C toppling like dominoes.

So after hours of dedicated trying, I give up and try to concentrate my mind on both healing and making the most of the two days that I have left. As soon as my bum heals, anyway.

Who knows, maybe it'll become an asset, my

bruised back end. Aren't there monkeys in Africa that use theirs as a warning beacon to ward off predators?

Maybe I made that up. I don't know. I don't know much about anything any more. Maybe I'm just going out of my head with boredom.

But what I do know is that I'll fight back from this. And if I can clobber Dyl along the way?

Then.

Bring.

It.

On.

There were two full moons last night. One shining down outside the tent, and a swollen one inside, keeping me awake, along with the hyenas and bears snuffling around outside.

But as the sun kicks the moon into touch, I make my mind up to be positive.

We've got two days left, and I'm not going to let damaged cheeks or a mentalist brother spoil either of them.

So I'm up first, exiting the tent without tripping (result) and getting to the toilet tent before anyone else can do something unthinkable in it.

On the way, I bump into Miss D.

"You all right Danny?" She smiles, but not in an "I'm laughing at you" way. It's clearly more of a "you poor thing having a ravaged bum and a psycho for a brother" kind of way. Which I appreciate. And agree with.

I only nod though. I'm happy to rant about Dyl, but don't really want to get into a conversation about the other bit. I'd rather pretend that it never happened, and I imagine Miss D feels the same.

Anyway, I'm about to push on to find a real bona fide dock leaf, when she does the kindest thing imaginable, the kind of thing that sums up why she completely and utterly rocks. She hands me a packet of tissues.

"I thought you might not be in the mood for foraging this morning." She winks, and moves on, leaving me to murmur, "Thank you," while trying not to blub like a fool.

And, you know what? That spurs me on even

further. I practically skip into the loo (being careful not to face-plant into the bucket) and emerge feeling like I could climb anything put in front of me.

Breakfast is next and I manage to pull enough milk from Flossy without giving myself blisters, and we even have time for a Jonny classic, when Geri reveals a load of hens living in the next field, ready to gift us eggs to cook.

Jonny, though, looks terrified and blurts, without thinking, "But how on earth do you milk a chicken?"

Now I don't want to sound harsh, but it's the funniest and daftest thing I've ever heard in

my life, and it gives me confidence, cos I know that for the rest of the day people won't be just giggling about my idiocy.

So when Geri tells us about what the day holds, I am properly bang up for it.

"MORNING, TROOPS," she barks, with an impressive enthusiasm for someone who fought in the Battle of Hastings. "I hope you slept well, because today is going to be a challenge. Tomorrow, we will embark on our final expedition, so to harden your resolve and put muscle on every bone in your body, I am going to test you. First of all, armed only with a compass and map, you will be orienteering—"

"What's paper folding got to do with anything?" Giraffles whispers, deadly serious.

"That's origami, you nugget."

"Oh right," he says, though I know he's still none the wiser.

"Trekking from this point, and avoiding any obstacles in front of you, you will proceed to

142

the river, where we will pick up kayaks to sail to a checkpoint. There, you will find a feast awaiting you. There will be challenges, there will be tears, but by the end of it, every single one of you will feel like a champion. So good luck … and steel yourselves."

We turn to a pile of alien-looking equipment to our left, confused looks on our faces. First, there are a series of square metallic boxes, with glass screens and a map inside. At least I think it's a map. It just looks like a load of random squiggles and shapes to me.

Lucky picks one up and stares at it, flipping it round and frowning.

"What are you looking for?" I ask.

"The serial number," he says. "It looks ancient. And this is either a well old model or it's just not working."

"It's not an iPad, you fool. It's a map in a Perspex box," I tell him.

"Yeah, I knew that." He blushes, though he's not the only one to make the same mistake. I swear I see Jonny pinching at his screen with his thumb and index finger, trying to make the map bigger.

I choose not to tell him though. I don't want to draw attention to him when he's still blushing about milking a flipping chicken.

Next to the maps are a load of clear plastic blocks, smaller this time so they fit snugly in your hand, with lines coming off them and the letters N, E, S and W.

"These are them things from Star Trek," blurts Marcus.

"Yeah," adds Maureen, "Kirk speaks to that Scottish fella on them, the one who's always blowing up the engine on the ship."

"BEAM ME UP, SCOTTIE!" they both shout into the plastic.

"Hhhhhhm, unlikely," says Giraffles, though he's clearly no idea what they do either, and I only know cos I've seen Dyl messing with one after he's been to cadets.

144

"It's a compass," I say, "it tells you which way to go: North, South, East, West … you know…"

They shrug, bemused.

"Explorers use 'em."

They shrug again.

"It's like satnav…" I add.

"Ahhhhh," they nod, all three idiots together. "I seeeeee… So where's the power button?"

I could, at this point, shake my head and walk away in disgust, but I remember how supportive they were over bumgate. If they laughed, they at least didn't do it to my face. So I grin through clenched teeth and explain how it all works, in brilliant, clear detail.

I tell them about how the earth is a huge magnet and how the north end of the compass is drawn to align with its magnetic field. I do it brilliantly, in fact I feel like a teacher, like how Miss D must feel, all smart and proud.

And do you know what they do?

They laugh at me, and tell me the nettles

must've rotted my brain.

So I do the decent thing, and tell them
something they will believe.

"No, you're right. Harry Potter invented them.
Or Dumbledore did at least. It's all magic."

"Sounds more likely," Giraffles adds, and
the other nod.

Maybe it's going to be harder to stay positive
than I thought...

And so we're off, though where we are actually off
to isn't quite so clear.

I can see the river on the map, but between
us and that point, there are a LOT of squiggly
lines that look like they've been drawn
excitedly by a toddler who's just eaten the
BIGGEST bag of sweets.

Bemused by where to even start, we do what
any novice explorers would – we watch what
direction Dylan heads off in, and follow him.

He's chosen to work on his own (no surprise

given the fact that he's a power-crazed meat head with only one friend, who happens to live in a mirror), and despite the fact that he's only on this bloomin' trip to supposedly look after us, he clearly wants to get there first and win the race. Which he will of course, because he's the only one who knows that the compass wasn't actually invented at Hogwarts.

Within two minutes, though, he's out of sight and we're left to flip between staring blindly at the compass, and then the map.

Our group is bigger than what is probably sensible. There's me, Giraffles, MandM, Lucky, plus Jonny, who I took pity on when no one wanted him in their group. After two minutes, I can kind of understand why.

"OOH. OOH. OOH." he shouts suddenly, after almost sticking his nose into the map. "Here," he points. **"HERE HERE HERE! WE HAVE TO GO HERE."**

Giraffles is irritated already. "I think Jonny might have spotted something he likes."

I give him a gentle dig and ask Jonny what he's seen.

"It's the answer to everything," he beams. "Look, the map says 'FB'. Right there. And you know what that means, don't you?"

"No," we all reply, as one.

"Well, 'FB' stands for Facebook, doesn't it? So there must be a phone mast there, where we can pick up a signal. We could call a cab to give us a lift to the river. We might even get there before Dylan."

Now I'm no expert, but somehow I don't think Jonny's got that quite right, so I open the map, and look for a list of what the symbols mean.

"Yeah … well, it's a nice thought, mate, but 'FB' means footbridge…"

Cue multiple cries of, **"YOU NUMPTY!"** from the others. At Jonny, not me.

"And before you ask," I add, "That 'i' isn't an iPhone charging point either. It means information."

But Jonny isn't disheartened by this. If anything

he looks chuffed. "Maybe the people there can order us a cab then. They might even have wifi, you never know."

I walk on, before the temptation to bury his head in a pile of leaves gets too great.

We wander on for ages, and it doesn't take long till people start bickering about which is the right way. Even MandM disagree on whether left is best or not, which makes me realize just how flipping lost we are.

But then, just when all hope is lost and I consider sending up an SOS flare (well I do till I realize we clearly don't own one), we see hope up ahead.

It's Dyl, about fifty metres to our right.

"What's he doing there?" I ask.

"Maybe he's lost too?"

"Impossible," I say. "He's way too annoying to ever let that happen."

"I don't even care," say MandM together. "I'm following him."

150

So we all do, except I do it way more cautiously than the others, because the difference is, I know him. I've had eleven years as his brother, so I know full well that he would NEVER let us follow him ... unless he was up to something.

"Nettles were just a starter," I say out loud without even realizing. "And whatever main course Dyl's cooking up, I ain't eating it."

The others look at me like I'm a loon and plough on, no matter how loudly I warn them, so I stay a step behind. If they want to walk into his trap, then they can do it first, not me.

It doesn't take long to be proved right either. We push on through a particularly thick piece of forest: it's dark, with endless branches blocking out the light.

"It's OK," says Giraffles, hacking at the last bits of undergrowth with a stray dead twig, "We're nearly through the worst of it."

These turn out to be famous last words for, as he swishes at the last branch, he triggers a booby

trap and up from nowhere springs the most evil-looking scarecrow you have ever seen in your flippin' life. It's naked, for starters, which doesn't help, but somehow, in practically no time at all, Dyl has built a figure entirely out of branches and twigs, all tied together with ivy. It stands over two metres high and, despite having no face, it is the scariest thing I have ever seen: its long arms loom over us like a zombie.

"**ARGGGGHHHHHH!**" cries Giraffles.

"**NOOOOOOOOOOOOO!**" yell MandM, while Jonny breaks wind with such a savage blast that I know it's the worst kind of fart: the liquid kind.

But I don't flinch, parp or even blink. I'm prepared. I have seen evil every day of my life, so when it appears, I'm ready for it.

"You'll have to do better than THAT, Dylan!" I yell into the trees.

And for the next twenty minutes, he tries his utmost: things tap us on the shoulders, but when we turn round there's no one there; we're pelted with acorns from all angles, but when we try to throw back there is no one to aim at; our ears are peppered with calls and wails that could either come from the most ferocious, dangerous animals on the planet, or from the lips of the biggest irritant that ever slimed his way across the earth.

By the end of it, even I'm starting to feel edgy, until I see, like a mirage in front of me, a break in the tree-line, and beyond it a pile of kayaks, and, even better than that, I can hear the faint gurgling of a river (which makes me instantly need a wee, but it's OK, I can live with that).

I break into a dance of joy, somewhere between the floss and the sort of dancing your mum does at a wedding disco after too many glasses of wine, and I skip towards the clearing. I don't care if I'm first or not. I don't care if I get a kayak with more holes in it than a cheese grater. All I care about is not falling foul of Dylan … again.

And it's actually that last thought that stops me

dancing. It's that thought that makes the others stop dancing too. Instead I hold my arms out wide to stop them getting past me.

"Wait!" I whisper.

"What?" they reply.

"It's too easy. There's no way Dyl would let us get to the end without nailing us. He's too evil for that…" And that's when I see it. The most pathetic excuse for a disguised trap ever.

There, on the floor, right on the edge of the wood, is a huge rug of twigs, dead branches and leaves. And the second I see it, I know that lurking below is a Danny-shaped hole, dug by my own brother's hands.

It's so obvious and so pathetic that I laugh out loud, in fact I howl, bent double with my hands on my knees.

"I've seen through you – you and your rubbish, pathetic trap!" I shout.

And with the greatest of care, I lead my friends around the side of the "pit" to safety, and towards

the majesty of the river.

But, in that one simple side-step, I realize my fatal error: the blanket of twigs left for me, is simply that. A blanket. There is no pit beneath.

I realize this when my feet are suddenly whipped out from beneath me, and I'm sent whizzing skywards and upside down, attached to a bungee rope that Dyl has hidden beneath a dense coil of ivy.

The blood races to my head, and it's a buzz, 'course it is. How could being thrown thirty metres in the air not be? But it's not the buzz I wanted. And although the view from the top of the tallest tree should be epic, it is most definitely not. Because all I can see as I look down is my big brother, laughing his bits off. And others in my class joining in too.

21

Nothing stops your bum stinging like being unexpectedly thrown thirty metres into the air. Honest, it's true. It makes your pride throb a bit, though.

Everyone had a right good laugh, until they realized it wasn't going to be so easy to get me down, and Geri had to climb up to make sure I didn't fall on my head.

Can't say it did a lot for my confidence, listening to her electric skeleton whirring its way towards me. No one really wants to be rescued by a person fifteen times their age, do they?

Still, better her than Dylan, and, believe me, he volunteered only to be shot down by an icy glare from Miss D.

They couldn't pin it on him, of course. There was no CCTV out in the back end of nowhere, and Dyl is as good at lying as he is at being a scumbucket.

Put it this way, if it was his job, he'd be a billionaire by now.

Anyway, to cut a long and devastatingly embarrassing story short, I ended up getting a piggyback down off Geri, before she took Miss D aside for a chat.

This just makes me feel even worse.

I mean, it's not my fault my brother is a psycho. Why can't he single someone else out instead of me?

This, and the nettle fiasco only happened to me – and who knew how long it would take before I was singled out again?

I tried not to think about it as I munched on a soggy egg sarnie, but wasn't helped by Miss D, who calls me aside.

"Danny, I'm worried."

"Me too," I say.

"I need you to stay away from Dylan."

"Believe me, I'm trying!"

"I appreciate that, but I need you to try harder. Now, I really don't know what's going on between you, but I've just had Geri in my ear, and she is more than a little concerned."

"Then tell Dyl, not me, Miss!" I plead. "He's tricking me, again and again."

"I'm telling you the same thing I've already told your brother. The reputation of the school is on the line. But, more important than that, I have to keep you all safe. And I can't do that if you and Dylan are engaged in some kind of deathmatch."

"But, Miss—"

"But nothing. Give him a wide berth, Danny, that's all I'm asking."

There's nothing I could say to that, but it was still on my mind as Giraffles and me clambered into our kayak, ready for phase two of the day. The only positive was that I stopped thinking about it as soon as I sat down in the cold, wet boat. My bum cheeks hurt too much for me to worry about anything else.

Turns out Giraffles had things on his mind though.

"Er, Geri," he says apologetically. "Shouldn't we be wearing life vests or nothing?"

Seems sensible to me.

Geri, however, thinks otherwise.

"My dear boy, I've been bringing recruits down this river for decades now, and I've never lost a soldier yet. Should you fall out, just swim to the surface. You can swim can't you?"

Giraffles nods, and that's all Geri needs to move swiftly on.

"The mission is a simple one. Navigate your way downriver as quickly, BUT AS SAFELY as possible," (and I know this is aimed at me), "and there are two things that you need to avoid at all costs. Firstly, this river is a nesting ground for the lesser-spotted, orange-crested warbler, a bird whose numbers have been falling in recent years. It is critical, CRITICAL, that you – like any good intrepid explorer – respect their habitat and do not disturb their nests! This is an important time for their young and, without them, the orange-crested warbler has no future."

There's a concerned murmur amongst the ranks, until Jonny pipes up with,

"What colour are they, Miss? So we know what to look out for?"

Honestly, if he keeps going on like this we'll

163

have enough material for a book before we get home. Geri very sensibly pretends he doesn't exist and carries on to point two, which is...

"Rapids! They're called that for a reason—" Jonny goes to open his mouth, but isn't quick enough.

"—And that's because, they are quicker and more deadly than any rollercoaster you've ever ridden. These rapids here would test even the most accomplished of adrenaline junkies, so I'm telling you now: stay clear of them. They are well signposted, so if you like your limbs attached to your bodies then keep your senses about you and do what the signs tell you. Now, go well, look after your partner, and we'll see you at the final checkpoint."

As warnings go, it's pretty clear, and as me and Giraffles push out from the bank I'm in no doubt about the fact that I'll be doing two things:

1. Exactly what Geri and Miss D told us
2. Not letting our Dylan anywhere near me

As long as I do that, there's no way he can

stitch me up.

And at first, this goes to plan. In fact, it goes better than that, because guess what? Me and Giraffles turn out to be kayaking heroes. This could, of course, be all down to my long-limbed mate and his epically telescopic arms that propel us downriver at a wild pace, but I'd like to think I'm doing my bit too, keeping us in rhythm and well away from the riverbank.

It's going so well that, actually, for a while we're at the front of the pack, waving to the imaginary crowds that line the bank. But after ten minutes or so, we feel two other kayaks drawing alongside us, and I know full well who one of them will belong to. It's Dyl, of course, which sets my heart racing and my bruised cheeks twitching. But then I see who's in the second boat and it's Geri, powering her twig arms (seriously, her paddles are more muscular) along at a furious rate. And that makes me feel way better, and safer too.

So we glide on, cutting the water in two,

giving even the quickest of fish below us a serious,
serious race.

Until…

"Hey, Danny. Look up there – that Dylan
waiting for us?"

I knew it. What he's done to Geri I've no idea.
Drowned her probably, or thrown her off the
nearest waterfall, before he does the same to me,
but as we draw closer, I see his plan up close and
personal, and it's obvious –
almost pitiful – what he's
trying to do.

"Look,
Giraffles," I say,
"look where he's
stopped. Right by
the sign to the
rapids."

He looks
and nods,
cos it's

true. Dyl has parked himself up at a small island in the middle of the river, where the water forks off in two different directions. And dug into the island is a wooden sign showing which way people go for the rapids.

Instantly, INSTANTLY, I am wise to his plan. **"I AM NOT FALLING FOR THIS!"** I yell, full of anger.

"Falling for what?"

"Isn't it obvious? He's changed the direction of the sign, hasn't he? He's pointed it in the wrong way, so we maim ourselves on the rapids. As soon as we go past, he'll change it back again so everyone else is safe."

"You sure?"

I look to my brother: my nemesis, my uber-archest enemy, put on this planet to make my life a living hell. His face is stony, giving nothing away. But at that moment I can see into his brain, can visualize the evil pumping around his bloodstream.

"I am positive. Certain. Sure."

"And he's definitely not trying to double bluff us?"

"That would involve his current brain cell having made a new friend. He thinks bluff means being naked."

"But if you take us down the rapids, you know we're going to impale ourselves on a rock, right?"

We approach the island, and the moment of decision is on us.

Left or right.

Right or left.

I look to Dyl, but his face gives nothing away. If I was searching the expression on his face for some kind of meaning, I'd simply think he needed a poo.

I look to my best friend. "He's changed the sign. I know he has."

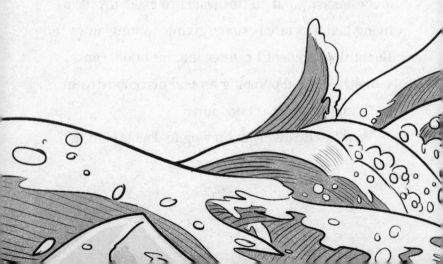

So we make a decision.

We steer left.

We pass Dylan.

And as we do he smiles slyly, waving with the very tips of his fingers.

Oh no.

We paddle on, and as we turn a corner the placid, mirror-like river disappears.

We appear to have steered into Niagara Falls.

We scream. Loudly. Wouldn't you?

22

22

I've never ridden the rapids before. Obviously.
The closest I got to it was when I was five and
had to share a bath with Dyl after a tea of beans
on toast.

And while that was distressing and scary, it's
nothing compared to this.

This is crazy stuff. There are waves bigger
than anything a surfer would dare tackle. And
there are bubbles. So many of them I reckon
Dylan dropped a bottle of washing-up liquid in
just to max the fear factor. So many of them it

makes it hard to keep your eyes open, especially when the kayak is writhing like a rodeo bull.

I try to row against the madness, thrusting my paddles in roughly, imagining the water's surface is Dyl's ugly mug, but it does nothing for our path or my anger.

Giraffles is doing his best too, his long arms clutching the paddles in the water, trying his best to steer us away from the rocks that jut out like mini-icebergs.

We miss one to our left, then another, then a third, on our right this time, but as we straighten up we see another, like a shark's fin haring towards us.

We scream and lean away, but we're going way too quick, which leaves us with only one option…

"Bail out!!"

I go first, but from the splash I hear, Giraffles doesn't need much persuading either.

Now, it may be spring, but nothing, NOTHING prepares us for the shock of the water as it blasts at our skin.

I kick to the surface and grab hold of the kayak. We can't lose it, and besides, I'm scared at where the next rock is coming from, so the boat is a handy shield.

"Grab on!" I yell at Giraffles, offering him the end of my paddle.

He hears me, and latches on. "Don't worry. I'll try to steer us towards the bank."

And he does as well – try, that is. But the only problem is that Giraffles, like giraffes, aren't known for their muscles. In fact, if they try to move quickly it often looks clumsy, like they only learnt how to walk twenty minutes earlier, and as a result of this we remain at the mercy of the rapids, buffeted and rocked from wave to wave, grimacing at the foam that peppers our faces.

Finally, we start to move towards the bank, giving us the chance to pull ourselves back on board, but as soon as we are sat back up, there are huge clumps of reeds and overhanging branches, at least thirty metres long, just waiting to gouge at us as we hare by.

"Brace yourself!" I yell, knowing it will be a lot easier for me to duck out of harm's way than my long-necked pal, but as we career towards the bank, yet another obstacle appears, as three startled birds skitter from the undergrowth. Three birds, each with the brightest orange chests I have ever seen.

"The lesser spotted orange-crested warbler!" shouts Giraffles, and at that moment I'm so pleased he's my co-pilot and not Jonny, who would probably have been screaming "ELEPHANT!" by now.

It's still bad news though. Really bad. Geri was clear: do NOT disturb their nesting area, at any cost, and here we were, bombing into it like a speedboat.

The reeds and branches envelope us, all we can do is close our eyes, try and stay the right way up, and not kill any birds…

"You alive?" I ask as we come out the other side, eyes still closed. I literally daren't look.

"…Kind of!" says Giraffles, though he sounds

… weird.

I allow my eyes to open, only to be hit by the most ridiculous of sights. Our kayak seems to have been transformed into some kind of bird sanctuary. From its tip to the cockpit, it is nest after nest after nest – and they're not empty, either. Each of them are chock-full of orange-bellied birds, adults, babies … there are even bloomin' eggs teetering about as the waves continue to crash over us.

"What have we done!?" I scream. "These nests fall overboard, and we could wipe out the entire population. Geri will kill us!"

I look to Giraffles for the first time since emerging from the reeds, and at first I think he's ditched his helmet for a weird elaborate hat, like one of those bonnets that they used to wear at Easter in the olden days. Then I realize it's not a bonnet at all. It's a nest, and there are two angry-looking orange-crested warblers flying round his head, presumably convinced that Giraffles is trying to kidnap their babies. And what's worse, they seem to have spotted me too, as have their friends.

Next thing we know, we're inundated, wafting them away from our faces like they were a swarm of killer bees.

It's awful, it's terrible, I'm cold, I'm wet and my bum hurts. This is, without doubt the final-est of final straws, and it makes me shout a sentence I never thought I'd shout:

"GET ME OUT OF HERE!!!!!"

23

It's darker than dark when me and Giraffles get back to camp. So late that even the campfire has given up, smoking lazily instead of roaring a welcome.

There's precious little of the feast left over for our hungry bellies either, though from the piles of washing-up left for us to sort as part of our punishment, it's clear it was quite a feed. Thick, meaty stew and rice, by the looks of it, plus a sticky chocolate-coated banana, roasted in the fire before cream was stuck all over it. I'm so hungry that licking a few plates crosses my mind… Don't judge me.

Our afternoon wasn't quite so entertaining.

Geri went loopy when we arrived at the finishing line disguised as a bird sanctuary.

"THERE WERE TWO RULES AND YOU BROKE THEM BOTH!" she roared. "No rapids, and no disturbing the nesting birds, so what happened, hhhhm?"

I tried to speak, but it turns out it was one of those rhetorical questions, when someone doesn't actually want an answer at all.

"Firstly, you could've killed yourself. Those rapids would challenge the strongest of explorers, never mind a couple of empty-brained fools like you, and secondly, we're only allowed to ride this river on the proviso that we don't tamper with the delicate balance of nature. Didn't I tell you that the orange-crested warbler was in danger? Didn't I tell you that they were nesting and needed space? I did. So why, then, did you choose to camouflage your kayak not only with their nests, but with half of the population – AND more eggs than you'd find at an Easter parade!"

I tried to speak again, but as Geri tried to catch her breath, it was Miss D who butted in.

"So why did you both choose the rapids? Because I know you. I know you're not stupid."

"It was Dylan, Miss."

"Not this again! I told you very clearly to steer clear of him. So why couldn't you do that? What did he do this time? Did he point you the wrong way? Or tamper with the sign?"

My brain stung with the desire to lie and scream **"YES, BOTH OF THOSE THINGS!"** But I couldn't, could I? Cos it's not true, and cos, unlike Dyl, I have standards, which is a word he can't even spell, never mind understand. But I did have to stand my ground.

"He didn't exactly point us the wrong way, Miss, but he's been messing with my head ever since we arrived. There was the nettles on my wotsit, then he strung me upside down from that tree. Honest, Miss, all he wants to do is ruin everything for me! He won't stop until he breaks me!"

I wanted to see Miss D soften, not cos I was spinning her a line, but cos it was true and cos she knows what Dyl is like. She taught him too, back in the day.

But her cross face didn't change a bit, and Geri's hardened like a sandwich left out in the sun.

"I'm sorry, boys, but any kind of provocation doesn't excuse what you did. We are lent this river on trust, and after today I'd be surprised if we're ever allowed to set foot here again. And as for your future on the rest of this trip, well let's just say I've already checked train times home."

It felt like the world was ending in that second.

"You're … you're kicking us off the trip?" I asked.

"I can't have recruits putting others at risk. Tomorrow is our final expedition, the most dangerous yet, and what happens if you decide to go rogue then, hhhm? How many lives would be at risk if you decide to ignore orders at sixty feet from the ground?"

"We'll do anything, Geri, Miss, anything not

to go home."

I looked at both of them, pleading with every muscle, every cell in my body. "I'll wash up for the rest of the trip, I'll even clean the toilet tent, with my tongue if I have to, I'll do anything as long as you don't send me home…"

"I think the washing up will be enough," Geri grimaced. "But first, the three of us have to return all these nests to their rightful places. We can only hope that the eggs have not been damaged by your recklessness."

"We'll do anything, anything you say, and we're sorry."

I turn to Miss, even though it's not my fault. "I really am." And I meant it, and we did it. We returned the nests, although hanging out on thin branches across the river felt just as dangerous as riding the rapids in the first place. But we did it with a smile and "Yes" and "Thank you" and plenty of "Anything you say".

Even now it's midnight and I ache from

forehead to toe, and I'm still scrubbing pots in lukewarm water, I stay polite. And apologetic. So much so that at the end of the chores, when my eyes are closing, I hear the words I'm desperate to hear.

"Gentlemen, you have one more chance, but be warned: you are drinking in the last chance saloon. Don't mess this up, and don't let me down."

Relief floods my body. I'm too tired for elation, or even mild excitement.

Instead, I thank Geri and fall through the flaps into my tent.

I'm asleep before my head hits the pillow.

It's the last morning of our trip and we have a "big day ahead", though what that actually means none of have a clue. Doesn't stop everyone gossiping though.

"Am sure I saw quad bikes parked up in the next field…"

"I reckon we'll be canyoning…"

"Segways!"

Jonny goes to open his mouth but is shouted down before he declares he's seen Geri carrying an astronaut's helmet.

I don't mind what we do to be honest. There's no way Geri's going to let us go home without a proper bang, and I'm just relieved to still be here.

I give Dyl as much of a wide berth as I can, but I feel him looking at me and laughing, remembering how many times he's stitched me up, probably, and working out the next angle, the ultimate humiliation.

I milk the cow that he *isn't* holding in case he winds it up and it kicks me, and I do six loops of the toilet tent before stepping foot in it, just in case he's lurking, waiting to pull the whole thing down on top of me.

I'm not paranoid or anything – I'm just not taking any chances when it comes to today. In fact, it's a relief when Geri calls us together, though I daren't look her in the eye in case she takes it the wrong way and makes me ride Flossy to the train station.

"Recruits!" she barks, stood to attention, "By the end of the day, I will not be able to call you that any more. By the end of the day you will have shed this skin. By the end of the day, you will be dirty and barely able to keep your eyes open. But you will be soldiers and warriors, each and every one of you."

It's a rallying call, that's for sure, and I think I can see Dyl getting emotional to my right, the plonker. He probably reckons he'll be James Bond or something by nightfall.

"Your mission today is three-pronged," Geri continues. "It starts, with a climb: a tough, one-hour ascent up a granite rock face that will not forgive any mistakes. It will hurt. Your muscles will ache; your fingers will feel like they no longer belong to you. But you must persevere, as waiting for you in the clouds is a tree-top challenge that would test even the hoolock gibbons of Eastern Bangladesh.

You will be higher than any tower block in any city in the world, but you will have to navigate your way, branch to branch, before you can reach the final challenge: the single longest zip line this country has to offer. Clinging on for dear life you will hit speeds that would make a Formula One driver queasy. You will be travelling so fast the g-forces will blow your cheeks neatly behind your ears…'"

I feel my cheeks clench with nerves… and not the ones on my face.

"Only when you feel your feet back on terra firma, and the dizziness turns into pure euphoria, will you be a Wild Out graduate. Many have failed, but that is not an option for any of you today. We go home triumphant, and we go home together!"

All right, so it's a bit dramatic – like she's been watching DVDs of that fat baldy bloke who fought off Hitler while sticking the V's to everyone – but it does the job, and we fall in behind her, marching to the mountain, carrying ropes so long that it looks like we'll be climbing all the way to Mars.

By the time we reach the bottom of the rock

face, it actually feels like that might be the case. I can't describe how tall it is, because we can't even see the top. It creeps into a cloud that clings ominously to it.

"We've got to climb through the clouds?" Giraffles asks, though it'll only take five minutes for his neck to disappear into it.

"Into the unknown, Thomas, but the weather is fair… for now."

"For now?" I gulp.

"This valley has its very own climate. And the weather can turn in an instant. We will have to be at our very toughest should it decide to test us."

I say nothing more, though my Adams apple has

morphed into a grapefruit. It dawns on me that I've never done this before. The others have – they had a full day of it while I was nursing my bum cheeks – but for me, this is new territory. All right, I've climbed a few walls in my life, and fallen off way more than I'd like, but this is... different.

It's scary.

And it only gets scarier as I watch my friends spider their way up, struggling to get a hold of the mountain's rough face.

I wait, and I exhale, trying to hold my nerve, until my time comes, and Geri attaches a rope to my harness, and barks the order:

"Climb, Danny Mack. Climb."

25

Fifteen minutes in and I know three things:

1. I am tired
2. I am not a mountain goat
3. There's nothing more demoralizing than being outclimbed by a woman old enough to be a caveman's grandma

I don't know where she gets her energy (or her robotic limbs) from, but I wouldn't mind a phone number so they could sort me out too.

Everything hurts,
from my fingers that
cling to the rock, to my
arms (working muscles
that I'm sure don't even
exist), right down to my
toes that have to wedge
themselves into crevices to
stop me falling backwards.

"Use the power in your
legs, Danny," Geri says.
"They're stronger than
your arms, so use them as
levers to push you up."

I try, honest I do, but I
think all of Dyl's torture
must've sapped me in
some way. Removed
my life force. I used to
think I was a Jedi, and
although I'm definitely

feeling greener than Yoda, that's definitely where the comparison ends.

I cling to the rock, craning my neck to look above, and see everyone else practically skipping up. Giraffles is covering ten metres with every stretch of his arms, MandM are climbing side by side, arms and legs moving together so smoothly that they look like some kind of weird mutant spider. Lucky, I swear, is singing as he goes, and even Jonny seems to be nailing it just by not saying anything stupid for a while.

"I can do this," I say to myself, "If they can do it, then I can too." And I dig in, stretching my fingers to a good handhold, listening to Geri as she tells me again and again to, "plot your path in advance. Like you're playing chess."

Chess? Right now I doubt I could win a game of noughts and crosses, and this is proven by the fact that the piece of rock in my hand is even more tired than me and comes away from the mountain, leaving me to topple backwards.

I make a noise that I have no idea how to spell, and grapple at the wall for some kind of safety, but it offers nothing and instead I fall, my stomach clenching, and my entire being screaming in fear.

I don't know how to describe how it feels to fall, except it's like I'm plummeting for minutes instead of seconds before the safety brake kicks in and I'm thrown into a hug with the rock, which doesn't offer much sympathy in return.

It hurts.

A lot.

Not that I see much in the way of sympathy from Geri, either, although the others shout support from above.

"The clock is ticking, Mr Mack," she says, and I see her frown doubly when she looks above.

"What is it?" I ask.

"Nothing," she replies, though her forehead is yelling LIE. "Keep moving, soldier. That's an order."

I know better than to ask any more questions,

and attach my grip back to the rock to start again, trying to remember everything she's already told me.

Progress is slow and painful, and now I daren't look up *or* down. It's too depressing to see my mates so far ahead, and too flippin' terrifying to see how far away the ground is. So instead, I focus on my hands above me, watching as the exertion turns my fingers blue.

"Come on!" I say through gritted teeth, "don't let Dylan beat you."

And you know what? I find a rhythm. It might only be the rhythm of a watch whose battery is dying but it's a rhythm all the same, and it's mine. Metre by metre, ledge by ledge, I edge slowly upwards, and I feel my confidence grow. I start to feel almost a little bit proud, like I want my mates to see I'm catching them up, so I look up, finally, ready to shout, but…

They've gone.

I can't see a single one of them, and I know

they've not fallen as they would've taken me with them. Instead, they've been eaten by the cloud. Except it's not like any cloud I've ever seen before, and it's definitely not the light fluffy one that was casually hanging around when we set off.

This one is dark, and heavy, uglier even than Dylan. And the second I see it, I know what Geri had been staring at worriedly. You don't have to be a weather woman to know what's lurking inside it, or the fact that it means trouble for us all.

"Er, Geri?" I offer.

"No time for chitchat, Danny. Keep climbing."

I don't say another word.

I have a feeling I'm going to need every breath in my lungs.

Do you ever imagine what it's like inside a cloud?

Cos I do, and I'll tell you something: I never imagined it would be like this.

It's not light, or airy. There aren't birds relaxing on plump, airy cloud-pillows, snacking on worms and singing to each other.

It's dark and damp, and it's hard to even see where your fingers are, never mind whether they're attached to the rock that'll stop you falling. The air is cold. It clings to my face and hands, but there's no way of warming up my fingers or any other part of me. Apart from by climbing. The faster I climb, the speedier the blood flows, and the warmer I'll get.

I don't need Geri to tell me this, either. I'm smart enough to do the maths, no matter what my brother might tell you.

So I double my efforts – triple them even. Put every bit of muscle that I have into it, no matter how much it hurts.

And I go up, up, up.

Then, from somewhere above, sweet music. Not the birds cheeping, but a Giraffles shouting.

"Danny? Danny mate, that you?'"

I squint through the cloud, dampness hugging my face.

"Yeah! Where are you?"

"Straight up, see? Here. At the top!"

I squint, but it's really thick now, like in one of those films where a cloud swallows everyone alive. Except when you're watching the film, you know it's fake and your mouth's full of popcorn.

All I can taste at the moment is fear, and it's neither sweet nor salted.

"Keep looking," he yells, "I can see you. Just. And keep going. You're nearly there!'"

That's all I need to hear to propel me on, and I power up, even shocking Geri, who doesn't look as in control as she usually does. In fact, for the first time since we've met her, she looks her age, which at the moment seems to be pushing a hundred and seventy-two.

"Here," says Giraffles, no longer needing to shout. "Reach up…" and I do, feeling two hands hoist me roughly over the rocks, not that I feel it – there's too much adrenalin coursing through my body. It's just a relief to know that I'm not going to die on that mountain's face, though judging by the expressions of the others huddled around me, we might be about to freeze to death whilst sat at the top.

"How long have you been waiting?" I ask Giraffles.

"Not long, really. Soon as the cloud dropped,

everyone slowed down. Can't believe how cold it is; it's not even bloomin' winter."

"No one ever said it would be easy!" booms Geri behind us, slicing through the cloud like an elderly robotic ninja. "This is the life of a soldier. Now sit together. Huddle close and preserve heat. Eat, refuel, then we move on."

"Er, Geri…?" asks Jonny, and we wait for his latest piece of brilliance. "Shouldn't we, you know, go back down? The weather's a bit … scary, innit?"

Mouths open, jaws drop. I swear that somewhere in the distance I hear an angel sing HALLELUJAH! because, you know what, Jonny's speaking something resembling sense, isn't he? It's dark, it's cold and its foggy so calling it quits and heading down to safety and a steaming mug of hot chocolate make sense to a lot of us. MandM have already stood up and are attaching themselves back on to the ropes.

Geri, however, has other ideas.

"Down? Down?! There is no down. Well, there is, but we can't go down the way we came up. Because none of you know how to abseil, do you?'

Heads shake. A lot of us don't even know what the word means…

"Can't we get a helicopter to fetch us?" asks Lucky, whose dad probably has a couple tucked away in the garage.

"Or an eagle with a saddle," adds Jonny helpfully, which makes Geri even more determined to push on.

"If we move quickly and with togetherness, we will be fine. This weather wasn't forecast so I'm sure it will clear quickly. Trust me."

And we do. Course we do. Cos, to be honest, there isn't another choice…

For fifteen minutes, we stumble along the rock face, hoods up and mouths closed. It's greasy underfoot, like someone's poured washing-up liquid under our trainers, and there's the constant echo of shouts as, one after another, children fall flat on their bums.

"GET UP!" yells Geri, every time. **"GET UP, AND GET ON!"**

But that's easier said than done, because the weather decides that instead of clearing up as she demanded, it's going to dig its heels in and stick its tongue out in the worst way imaginable.

It starts with a huge rasping raspberry of a wind that comes from nowhere, battering our faces and whipping at our waterproofs.

"It's OK," shouts Geri, "this is good! The wind will blow the clouds away quicker. The sun will be out in no time."

But the weather is obviously listening and – oh boy – it does not like Geri, because it reaches into its huge bag of tricks and throws a belter of a weapon straight into her face.

Rain.

And not just the pittery-pattery variety.

No, this is rain that has been sharpened into

tiny, lethal arrowheads and spat, in its thousands, directly into our faces, forcing us to hunch over to protect our eyes, while struggling with the treacherously slippy rock beneath our feet.

"Move quickly but carefully. The woods are only two hundred metres ahead!" Geri squeals, barely loud enough to beat the sounds of our complaints.

But, the woods might as well be two hundred miles away, cos the weather hurls the double whammy of rain AND wind at us, and it's a murderous act with disastrous results.

Many of us are on the small side, and as a result don't weigh an awful lot. Jonny in particular would barely trouble a set of scales, but he's not the one most affected by the gusts hammering us.

Geri is.

I see it first, but can barely believe my eyes…

"Giraffles, oh boy, look! This isn't good…"

"What is it?" he replies, not wanting to raise his face to the daggery rain.

"The wind. It's lifting her. It's lifting her up…
off her feet!'"

And it is, I swear it is. I don't know how, cos
after all, Geri is part cyborg, and surely cyborg
skeletons weigh more than human ones, no
matter how old.

But obviously they don't, as no matter how
hard she tries, Geri is repeatedly plucked
momentarily from her feet, before being dropped
to the ground.

There is a yell. A yell of pain. But it doesn't last
long, as Geri's pain seems to turns to fear. The
greasy rocks starts to tilt away from her like a
slide, and with the rain and the wind still swirling,
she moves away from us, quicker and quicker.

Away from us, and closer and closer to the edge
of the mountain that we've just climbed.

"Miss!" Giraffles and me squeal as one, but
Miss is bringing up the rear and too far back to
do a thing.

All we can do is watch through our hands,

as our leader and guide hurtles, quite literally, towards the abyss…

27

Time does not stop still, or slow down.

Not even close.

Everything speeds up, especially Geri, her thin bones skidding over the rock like she was riding a bobsleigh.

We watch as she grapples for something to hang onto, anything that would take the edge off the pace she's motoring at.

Tree roots offer a bit of help, but no matter how strong her robotic hands are, they aren't tough enough to hang on for longer than a few seconds, and she's left to ricochet on, powerless.

"MISS!" MandM yell, their two voices definitely better than one. But although Miss D has no problem hearing them, there is no way she can reach Geri in time to be any kind of help.

Dyl neither: he's too busy trying to look like the weather isn't troubling him to realize it's troubling him too much to help.

And this is when something surprising happens. Giraffles sticks his neck out. Properly, for real.

Now, he's brilliant is G, and that's why he's my best mate, but he's not exactly known for his bravery. He'd run a mile if a spider spun a web within a hundred metres of him. But when he sees Geri flailing past us, something comes over him and those epically long legs of his ignore the wind and take off after her.

For the first few strides it looks completely pointless and weird, frankly, but that doesn't get in the way of him trying, and you know what, the gap starts to close.

212

"GERI!" he shouts. **"THERE'S A BOULDER! GRAB IT! PLEASE!"**

I see what he's shouting about, and there's every chance Geri will be able to do it. In fact, she has to, cos beyond that there's nothing else to grab except air. And although there's plenty of that between the cliff edge and the valley below, it's not going to be any help whatsoever.

Geri knows that too, she's a warrior after all, and so she digs deep, arms outstretched as the rock zooms closer.

Giraffles meanwhile, is still running along, or at least he was, because as Geri's fingers manage to make contact with the boulder, he flings himself head first on to the ground, sliding like a footballer does after they've just netted from the halfway line.

It's a bonkers decision, but given that I'm still rooted to the spot in fear, I don't question it, unlike Giraffles himself, who shouts at me over his shoulder.

"Danny, get the others. You need to grab my

legs, and don't you dare let go!"

It's not a plea we can ignore, and we belt after him, fast enough to reach his ankles without throwing ourselves into the abyss as well.

He's still on his belly, head pointing down to the cliff edge, arms stretching out for what looks like an eternity, in the direction of Geri, whose grip is loosening by the second. He glances back over his shoulder at us. "Hold on tight," he says. **"AND WHEN I SAY PULL, PULL!"**

With that, his attention flies back to our leader, and he barks instructions just like she has for the past three days. It'd be proper impressive if it wasn't so ridiculously scary, scary enough for Geri to do exactly what he asks, grabbing onto his hands with her own.

"PULL, DANNY, PULL!"

I don't need telling again, and
nor do the others. We yank at
Giraffles' elasticated legs, digging
our heels into the skiddy rock to
stop ourselves from toppling over.

Others join in, grabbing us from
behind and pulling too, till it feels
like we're the rope in an enormous
tug of war, so goodness knows how
poor Giraffles must feel.

He doesn't moan though, or if he
does we cant hear him as his head
is still face down in the dirt. But
we feel him slide closer and closer
to us, and see Geri
following close behind.

"Don't stop! Don't stop," screams

Miss D as she gingerly steps beside us, grabbing onto Geri's elbows as they slide into range.

We do what she tells us, and with one final tug, we all fall backwards into a pile, Geri catapulting to the top of the scrum, safe, but in pain, offering two words that none of us really want to hear.

"It's broken."

I hope she's not badly hurt, I really do, but I also hope she's referring to a small part of her body, rather than our way back down to safety...

28

"You all right there, Geri?" I ask, as we head as speedily as we can for the forest.

"Like I'm sitting on the comfiest sedan chair in the world," she answers with a grimace and a dollop of sarcasm.

I can't blame her. Last place I'd want to be when I'm nearly two hundred years old and have a smashed-up ankle is on my idiot brother's back, especially when he's revelling in the glory of being the saviour. Honest, I thought he was going to do a hundred press ups before lifting her for the first time, just to get his guns pumping and primed.

I rolled my eyes but said nothing. I wasn't going to give him any ammo after what he's done to me over the last few days.

"Keep going, recruits," Geri rallied, "as soon as we hit the trees the weather won't be half as bad."

"It couldn't get any worse, could it?" asks Lucky, his trademark smile missing from his face. He does have a point though: the tiny arrowhead raindrops have been replaced by a billion massive, bucket-sized ones, the type where a single drop would soak every centimetre of you more effectively than a waterfall.

Still, it drives us on, and finally, finally, we feel the trees take the brunt of the clouds instead of our heads.

"Well done, everyone!" beams Miss D, but the smile on her face looks more like relief than joy. "Not far now."

We know, though, that that is not strictly true.

There's still the walkways in the trees to pass through, and then the zip line – and how on earth are we going to get Geri through all that, cos although Dyl thinks he's strong, even he can't do it.

It's too much – even just the thought of it – there has to be another way. I pull my phone out of my pocket and stare at the screen.

No bars whatsoever.

"Anyone got a signal so we can ring Mountain Rescue?"

Hands reach into soaked pockets and phones appear, some better than others but none of them managing to reach a satellite successfully, not even Lucky's, which is so high-tech it should be able to morph into a helicopter and fly us down.

But just as our spirits sink once more, a lone voice cuts through the gloom.

"IT'S WORKING!" Jonny shrieks. **"IT'S ONLY BLOOMIN' WORKING!"**

I resist the temptation to shout, *What your*

brain? Finally! because he's looking at his phone, the screen lighting his delighted face.

"I've got a signal. Four bars. Count 'em, count 'em!" and he starts doing a little jig, which almost turns into a full on breakdance, and ends up with the phone slipping out of his fingers and onto the stony ground.

It bounces in slow motion, every one of us yelling **"NOOOOOOOOOOOOO"** as one.

Our hearts refuse to beat as he snatches it up, desperate to assess the damage.

"It's OK, it's OK – it's not smashed, it's not smashed."

"Just call the cops will you, Jonny?" Lucky demands. "Please!"

So Jonny bashes in 999, puts the mobile on speaker and then we hear the greatest words we have ever heard:

"999,"

YES!!!

"Which service do you requi—"

Then… nothing. Silence. And nothing on the screen either. The blue hue flicks to black, and it hangs limply in Jonny's hand, exhausted. Dead.

"My battery's died!" he says like his world has been snatched from him.

"Maybe if you weren't checking it every minute then you'd still have some juice left," Lucky shouts.

"It's not my fault, at least my phone got a signal before it died. Yours is rubbish!"

It goes on like this for a couple of minutes, the disappointment turning into frustration and then full-on anger.

But I don't join in. there's no point. Instead, I turn up the collar of my coat and walk on.

"Where you going, Danny?" Giraffles asks.

"Down. Home. Hopefully."

He nods and walks after me, and soon the others start to follow too.

29

I have always loved watching monkeys.
Gibbons especially.

Not that I've ever actually seen one,
obviously. We do have exotic breeds of vermin
back on the estate, rats mostly, but not much in
the way of monkeys.

I've seen plenty of them on the telly, though.
Seen how effortless they make it look, looping
from tree to tree, never pausing or thinking for a
second that they might fall to their death.

But it's only now I realize how rubbish we are

– humans – cos we aren't swinging from anything to anything. All we're trying to do is walk across slightly greasy wooden walkways. And we're even doing that badly.

We aren't even in Madagascar or Africa, we're just in the middle of nowhere, though we are completely soaked and utterly, utterly cheesed off.

The thought of cheese makes my tummy rumble. We've been making our way through the trees for over an hour now, and to be fair it's partly taking so long cos the planks under our feet are properly soaked, and they've collected all the muck off the rained-on leaves, which is making it feel like an ice rink.

On top of that there's thirty of us, and nobody ever needs to pee at the same time. And there are obviously no loos at the top of trees, or bushes either.

Oh, and our colonel has a mashed-up leg and needs carrying.

To be honest, it's a wonder we've managed to move at all.

But then a voice comes from the gloom.

"Well done, troops. You've almost made it. Look ahead and you'll see one last rope bridge for us to cross, before the final zip line down."

We squint into the darkness. And it really is dark, despite it only being mid afternoon. The trees are thick and dense, like something from the Amazon, and we can tell from the rain still puncturing its roof that the clouds are no better up above. If anything, it must be raining even harder.

"Can you see it?" Giraffles asks, "The bridge?"

"Yeah, up there. And to the right a bit." Though to call it a bridge may be stretching it a bit. Bridges are usually designed by engineers, aren't they? Who go to university for half a lifetime before they're trusted to make anything? This looks like it was designed by a seven-year-old in science class, then knocked together during a couple of wet lunchtimes.

It's long, probably thirty metres or so, with a big old dip in the middle, like an elephant's been napping there for the past eighteen months. My confidence in it doesn't grow as we move closer either. I can see that rungs are missing along it, and that the rope is fraying and straining in places, as if the storm has left it exhausted.

"It may look rickety, but trust me," says Geri, "it has stood for years that bridge, and it'll stand for many more." But there's that look on her face again, the one

she was wearing when she first saw the cloud falling over the mountain.

"This is how it works," she continues, "We cross the bridge in groups of three, as space on the zip wire platform is small. One by one, you will travel down the zip line, and the waiting passengers must wind the winch back up to the top in readiness for the next child. Got it?"

We nod and she smiles. "I know this has been difficult – a challenge even. But you have handled it admirably and I promise you, the dramas are over. Finished. Done."

Which is exactly when the thunder rumbles, scaring us half to death.

Maybe it's the weather gods laughing at Geri or maybe we are, actually, doomed,

but the storm doesn't hesitate. It tells us it means business: there's no rumbling in the distance, the thunder is on top of us already and the rain follows angrily, puncturing the last of the treeline and hammering on the rope bridge, making it shake with impact.

"Let's GO!" shouts Miss D, who I reckon will

now be sworn off school trips for the rest of her life, and we shuffle on, the impact of the rain on our shoulders and heads making us flinch.

Up close, the bridge looks no safer than it did from a distance, in fact it looks terrifying. But I keep the sight of the zip line in my mind. One more ride, I tell myself, one more ride and we'll be back on the ground. It looks like the others agree, as there's no shortage of volunteers to go first, no matter how shaky the bridge seems.

After much persuasion from Miss D, Geri goes with the first two, bum-shuffling across the wooden planks like she's done it a million times before, though I see the grimace on her face with every movement, the bridge creaking and buckling as she goes.

It seems to take an age for the first three to get over and Geri almost needs pushing down the zip line, not wanting to leave anyone behind. Passage across the gorge is slow, and while the zip line looks super speedy on the way down, winding the handle back up takes time and energy. All we can do as we wait is try and keep warm, though it's impossible to stay dry as the rain falls with greater and greater venom.

Minutes pass and the weather worsens – even the wind has picked up as well, presumably as it felt left out.

But we can't let it stop us, and slowly but surely there are less and less of us waiting on the wrong side of the bridge. In fact, there's six: me, Giraffles, MandM, Miss D, and Dyl of course.

"Right, Dylan," says Miss D, "you take Marcus and Maureen, and Danny and I will follow last."

But Dyl, in true annoying style, has to have the last word. "I'll wait with our Danny, Miss. With my training it makes sense for me to go last. I can fire fight anything that comes my way, no problem."

Honestly, the boy is so cocky. If he shoved his chest out any further he'd be pushing us off the platform and into the void.

"Are you OK with that, Danny?" she asks, and I nod, cos I am. What else is Dyl going to do, push me to my death? Can't see how he'd explain that one away to Mum.

So, with one final look over her shoulder, Miss D shepherds MandM across to the far platform, though how she manages to get them down the zip wire one at a time, I have no idea.

Five minutes later, and once her terrified tones dies away as the zip line whooshes to the ground, there's just the two of us left. Me and Dyl. Beauty and the Beast.

"Well then, little brother," he beckons, "shall we?"

And there's nothing else to say, except yes.

Except I don't get to say it, do I?

Cos that is the moment when the lightning strikes.

The noise is sickening, like the tree is screaming in pain as the lightning cuts it in two.

It splits slowly at first, but gets quicker as the tear gets deeper, and I realize quickly that although the tree was some distance from us, it would properly wallop us on its way down.

"DYLAN," I yell, all rivalry forgotten, **"JUMP! NOW!"**

But all he does, the plank that he is, is turn and look directly at it, eyes widening as it begins to plummet towards him. He's frozen. Rigid. And for the first time in my life, I see he's terrified.

"Dyl! JU—"

But there isn't time, and without thinking I jump straight at him, rugby-tackling him around the waist. I feel his legs give, and my momentum throws us sideways as I feel the rush of wind and vibrations of tree on earth. It's like an echo. People probably feel it all the way down in Australia.

As soon as the shaking stops, Dyl throws me aside with an embarrassed huff.

"Get off me, weirdo!"

"Oh I'm sorry, for a second there I thought I was saving your stupid life. Remind me to forget next time."

But I don't think he can hear me, as his eyes land on the fallen tree and we both see just how HUGE it is.

"Is that a redwood? I've seen them on the telly..."

"It's massive, that's what it is."

And we both realize, I think, just how close we were to being squashed flat by it. It. Is.

MAMMOTH. Cut it up and light it and you could warm a town for a good couple of years, not that we had any intention of breaking out a hacksaw.

All I want is to get back down to earth and get out of here.

But as I pull myself on top of the trunk, I see the worst thing imaginable. The tree has fallen across the gorge, and has completely trashed the rope bridge. There's not a plank or even a frayed rope to be seen.

There's a fresh crack of thunder and an immediate flash of lightning that lights our faces, and no matter how hard he tries to hide it, I know that Dyl is just as scared as I am. In fact, he seems more scared, cos his ability to think straight is gone.

"What are we going to do now?" he asks, and he looks younger, like a little kid who's just dropped his dinner money down the drain. I think he might be about to cry.

I know I could tell him to grow up, or ask him

what his extensive training would tell him to do, but I also realize in that instant that there's only one person who's going to get us down off this mountain, and it's not GI Joe whimpering over there. It's me.

So I look closer at the fallen tree. It's even bigger than I thought. Maybe, just maybe, it might have bridged the entire chasm itself, and if we're really careful we can just walk across it to the other side.

But no, that would be too bloomin' simple, wouldn't it? Because of the way that it's fallen, there's still a real gap between it and the zip wire platform. But what I don't know yet is whether we can jump the final bit.

I explain to Dyl that we need to find out, that one of us needs to shimmy along it to work out how far that jump would be, but when he pulls his soaked head so far inside his coat that he looks like a terrified turtle, I realize that person is me.

So off I go, to the edge of void, where the rope

bridge used to begin, and sit on the tree trunk,
a leg either side. What follows is clumsy and
embarrassing, as I make little bum jumps along the
bark, like a rabbit trying to scratch an itchy bum.

The movements are small, but it's solid. I
manage to make progress without dislodging the
tree or sending myself hurtling into the abyss.

Within minutes, that feel like hours, I'm far
enough along to be able to see clearly, and I
decide:

1. The gap is jumpable
2. The gap would be the biggest jump of my
life
3. I don't know if standing on the tree would
make it capsize, and send both of us to our deaths

It's not ideal, and the thunder and lightning
continue to spit rainy daggers in my direction.
How long till another zigzag hits another tree,
which wipes out our tree and makes it properly
impossible to get across?

There are too many things to worry about.

I bum-jump backwards (this should be an Olympic sport), until I find myself face-to-face with Dyl again.

"It's good news," I lie, leaving out my concerns about the tree toppling into the abyss. "There's a gap at the other end, but it's jumpable, especially for you."

That's not a lie, cos he's way bigger than me, and he's been jumping for years now (even if that is mostly on me).

He obviously isn't keen on the idea, but at the same time I can see he doesn't want to look scared in front of me, so after a bit of stalling he begins bum jumps of his own, which lack the technique I've developed but I see him reach the end of the tree in record time.

I watch from the bank, not daring to step on the tree in case the weight of us both is too much. The tension eats at me, as well as the wind and the rain and the constant threat of being deep-fried by a lightning bolt, and for a while I wonder if Dyl is going to jump at all, or whether the fear has totally grabbed him.

But then, just as I'm about to shout, he jumps, and I watch as the tree wobbles beneath him. For one horrible second I think momentum is going to make it tumble down, leaving me stranded. I even consider grabbing it and trying to hold it steady until I realize the weight of it could easily catapult me to my doom.

By the time I've made all these realizations, I see that Dylan has landed, safe and cocky, on the other side, and is already winching up the zip line. He probably wont even wait for me, why break the habit of a lifetime now?

As another rumble hits above me, I sit astride the trunk and shuffle my way along. The bark is wet and slippery, and I feel my hands slide off it on several occasions, testing my balance and my nerve.

I'm fighting off rain, wind and a dollop of low cloud, just to really test me, and it doesn't help when the tree trunk starts to groan and ache, reminding me that it is in no way happy about holding me like this. I ignore it and shuffle on, right to the very end.

The gap seems bigger than it did five minutes ago – five times bigger – and suddenly I'm not sat on a log but stood on a brick wall, back on the estate, and there are little kids laughing and pointing at me, and I don't know if I can do this anymore. I don't want to stand up. But I don't want to stay here either, especially as Dyl has hauled the zip line handle up to the top and is already fastening his safety line to it.

And you know what? By doing this, he does me the biggest favour, and I stand up instantly. I want him to see me make this jump, to see that no matter how many nettles rub against my bum, or how many times he traps me thirty metres in the air, he can't beat me. Cos I'm Danny Mack, and without me, his sad little life would've been squashed flat minutes ago.

But just as I make a mental note to remind

him of this every five minutes for the rest of our lives, there's an explosion from above. A crack of thunder, the loudest yet, and with it a blinding forked flash that zigzags behind me, hitting the exposed tree roots on which I'm standing. The trunk trembles with the impact, and there's a new noise, a sizzle, and I don't need to look over my shoulder to know that the tree is on fire.

"YOU'RE KIDDING ME!" I wail, because how can anything as wet as this tree still be catching fire? But from the smell, I know it's doing its very best.

So I do the only thing I can do: I look forwards, not at the gap between me and safety, but on the lip that I need to land on. I can do this, I tell myself. I'm a free runner, I'm an explorer, I'm a soldi—

And then the tree starts to give way beneath me.

I feel it tip and turn and know that the moment is now – I need to go, throw myself forward before the spinning log sucks me down into the gorge.

With every muscle and every sinew bursting,
I launch myself, eyes fixed on the ledge. Wind
whips my face and rain stabs at my eyes, but I
ignore it. I've done too much these last few days,
and had too many things done to me to fail
now, and with each centimetre I cover, I feel my
confidence grow.

"**ARGHHHHHH!**" I yell, arms
outstretched and braced, but the
momentum seems to stop, and
that forward motion morphs
into a downward one.
The ledge seems to
be further instead of
nearer, and I hear the
tree trunk give up its
fight as it topples head
first into the gorge.

I feel pain rip at my
fingers as they bite
into the stony ledge.

The rest of my body slams into the ridge below, bruising me instantly, but my fingers hold on.

I can do this, I tell myself, not even considering for a second about shouting for Dyl – he's probably zipping down the line by now anyway. I dig my toes into the wall, finding a crevice I can use as leverage.

I push, my legs straightening, my fingers on fire, until I can wedge my elbows onto the ledge instead. The wind gusts at me and pulls at my trouser legs, but I'm too close now to let it win, and with one final, monumental effort I swing my left leg up and onto the ledge, my body rolling with it, to safety.

Everything hurts – my hands, my ribs, my legs, my brain – but all I can do is laugh. I turn my head up to the clouds and I laugh myself silly, drinking the rain as I do so.

"You," Dyl sneers, "are a nutter. And don't even think about telling the others that you saved me up here. Cos let's face it, no one will believe you."

Tucking his legs up and clinging to the zip line, he begins his final, speedy descent, leaving me alone, at the top, laughing like a loon and feeling like the king of the world.

31

We wave at Geri from the window of the coach,
and she salutes back, perfectly balanced despite
the pot hugging her ankle and the crutches
wedged under her arm.

It wasn't an emotional goodbye – elderly
cyborg warriors don't tend to cry often, probably
cos it damages their wiring. The salute and the
smile said all she needed to say.

Miss D doesn't say a right lot either. She just
shakes her head endlessly, while whispering
something about "never again". Looks like she

could do with a hug, to be honest.

There's plenty of chat on the bus, though. Everyone's got a tale to tell, some of them true, a lot of them properly over-exaggerated. Everyone wants to be a hero, I suppose.

Me? Not so much. I haven't told anyone about what happened at the top of the mountain. Not because of what Dyl said – I don't care if people believe him over me. I know what happened and so does he, and we'll carry that over the next few days and weeks and months.

I am watching Dyl though, sitting a few rows ahead. On his own, of course.

And I'm watching him for a very good reason. Before we got on the bus, we had to make ourselves a packed lunch. And I managed to do a good thing. Well, for me at least.

I got my old mate Giraffles to distract our Dylan, while I put on some gloves and swapped the wild rocket in his sandwich for something equally green, but way more spicy.

I've never eaten nettles, but I hear they carry quite a kick. It might be a while before he gets hungry, but that's OK. I can wait.

I turn my head and look out the window as the countryside rolls past.

There are fields and mountains and pylons as big as iron giants, and in the distance, there's a big old beast, grazing on some grass.

I look at Giraffles and MandM and Lucky and poor old Jonny, and we point, and smile, and say, all at the same time...

"LOOK! A RHINO!"

And then we laugh so hard we think we'll never laugh again.

Until, that is, our Dylan, opens up his lunch box...

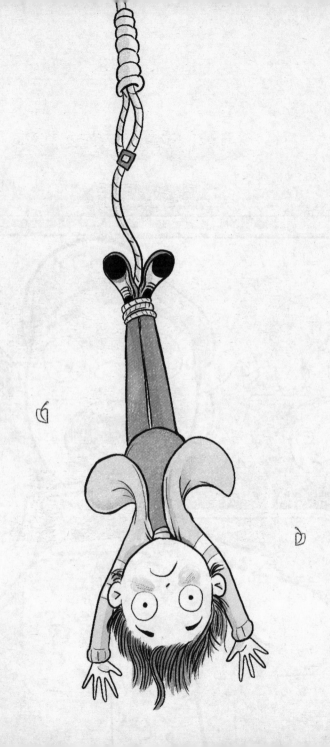

QUESTIONS WITH

WITH

ANDY

AND

PHIL

1. DID YOU GO ON SCHOOL TRIPS WHEN YOU WERE A KID?

ANDY: I can remember just the one. I was in primary school and we went to Crystal Palace Park to see the life-sized concrete dinosaurs. I never went on any other school trips because normally parents had to pay, and my parents didn't have the money to do so. But it was OK because there were lots of kids whose parents couldn't pay, so it felt sort of normal and we became a bit of a gang.

PHIL: Yes, but they were nowhere near as cool as the one in this book. We got to walk across the Humber Bridge (yawn). At the end of it you were given a commemorative spoon... To this day I have no idea why!

2. WERE YOU USED TO THE COUNTRYSIDE AS A KID? WHAT DO YOU REMEMBER ABOUT IT?

PHIL: I grew up in Hull, which has plenty of green areas but it is the flattest place on earth. The first proper hills I ever saw were in the Lake District, and it took my breath away (even before I started walking up them). I live in the hills now, and wouldn't live anywhere else. I love it.

ANDY: I was maybe ten or eleven years old when I first saw the countryside. I went with my dad to a place near Portsmouth called Cowplain, because he had to collect some furniture from an uncle there. I had never seen a cow before and was disappointed as there were only houses in Cowplain, so, while my dad loaded the furniture, my auntie drove me out to the countryside to see some cows. She explained how the milk came out of them, which was news to me. It was very exciting, as I didn't realize how big they were!

3. HAVE YOU CLIMBED MOUNTAINS? HAVE YOU EVER GOT LOST IN THE MOUNTAINS?

ANDY: Yes, it happens sometimes when the clouds come down low over the mountain and you can't even see in front of your nose. The last time this happened was when I was in the Black Mountains in Wales. The only thing to do is stop and keep warm and dry before trying to work out where you are. Only then can you start moving to where you want to be. If you keep moving while not knowing where you are, you become even more lost.

PHIL: I have. I've climbed, abseiled and walked up them, including in Peru, where I had the most embarrassing experience of my life … see below!

4. WOULD YOU KNOW HOW TO USE A MAP IF YOU GOT LOST?

PHIL: I wouldn't have a clue! I like to follow my nose...

ANDY: I learnt to read a map when I joined the army and it is still taught to all soldiers because it's so important. Technology can run out of power, it can get broken or lost when used out in the field. If that happens, soldiers have to go back to getting out their map and compass and going old school.

5. HAVE YOU EVER BEEN KAYAKING? AND DO YOU HAVE ANY TIPS ABOUT STAYING SAFE IN THE WATER?

PHIL: I have. I went sea Kayaking in Canada. We paddled out to a deserted island and slept out there. It was incredibly exciting.

ANDY: I haven't been kayaking, but I suppose the best way to stay safe in the water is to learn how to swim – and also to learn the skills to save others.

6. WHEN DID YOU LEARN TO SWIM?

ANDY: I learnt with mates at the local baths. We just messed about bombing each other and poor unsuspecting swimmers, and we sort of got the hang of swimming through trial and error!

PHIL: I learnt when I was young. It basically involved being shouted at by a man who was bitter that he wasn't quite good enough to go to the Olympics. I'm not a very good swimmer, and I absolutely blame him for it…

7. HAVE YOU EVER MADE A BIG JUMP AND FALLEN?

ANDY: Thousands of times! Falling isn't the problem; it's the last centimetre before hitting the ground when it starts to become painful.

PHIL: YES!!! About fifteen years ago, I went trekking in Peru. We were walking up to Machu Picchu, and on the first night we camped in a clearing on the edge of a mountain. Now I'm not a snob, but the toilet was exactly like the one in this book. It was a bucket with a bin-liner in. Oh my word … it STANK. And you could see what everyone had done in there before you, so I was desperate not to use it. That night though, before I went to bed, I needed a pee, so instead of using the toilet tent, I decided to walk off the clearing and wee in the trees. The only problem was, it was dark, and I walked off the edge of the mountain instead, and slid about forty metres down the cliff. It was properly, properly scary, and even more embarrassing, as the trek leader had to abseil down to retrieve me... I'm blushing even thinking about it.

8. HOW WOULD YOU DEAL WITH DANGEROUS TERRAIN, OR BEING SCARED?

PHIL: Probably really badly. I think I'll stick to writing about it.

ANDY: The best way is to avoid it if you can. Try going around it to get where you need to be. People think that being scared is weakness, but it isn't. Even boxers are scared but they call being scared "the gift of fear". Fear makes you more determined to get on with the task and succeed.

9. WHAT WOULD MOTIVATE YOU TO KEEP GOING WHEN YOU'RE TIRED, COLD OR HURT?

ANDY: There is nothing else to do but accept the situation you are in and just get on with getting out of it!

PHIL: Probably the thought of food at the end of it. Pie and chips, that should do it.

ACKNOWLEDGEMENTS

Huge thanks to Jodie, Emily, Philippa, Robin, Pete, Sam, Rachel, Beth and definitely Fiz who edited on the dash without ever breaking sweat!
– Andy & Phil

Big love to Albie, Elsie, Stanley, Louise (xx), Rufus, Bebe and Nancy. You lot make me proper happy – Phil